BREAK LIMA

A H FITZSIMONS

First published by eBookPartnership.com 2014
Paperback edition published by CompletelyNovel.com 2015
ISBN 978-1-8491452-3-7

Formatting and typesetting: Simon Hartshorne
Printed in the UK

Cover: MICHAL BARAN
Photograph: Washington Gwande
Model: Joy Fitzgerald

For Georgina and Christine

Contents

Great hope has no real footing unless one is willing to face into the
doom that may also be on the way.

Norman Mailer

BREAK LIMA

Introduction

Following the terrorist attacks of September 11, 2001, the CIA contracted two psychologists, James Elmer Mitchell and Bruce Jessen, to develop alternative, harsh interrogation techniques. The psychologists recommended use of the Air Force's Survival Evasion Resistance Escape (SERE) counter-interrogation training, reverse-engineered to obtain intelligence from captives. Their recommendations resulted in the formation of enhanced interrogation techniques which included waterboarding, hypothermia and stress positions. These techniques were employed routinely on terror suspects by the Bush administration. They were subsequently deemed unacceptable, as they were clearly methods of torture, comparisons being made to the Gestapo interrogation method called 'Verschärfte Vernehmung'.

Eight years prior to the September 11 attacks, with no sign of an end to the troubles in Northern Ireland, British Military Intelligence conducted an experiment designed to obtain information without the use of recognized methods of torture. The objective of the experiment was to subject a military volunteer to prolonged extreme stress, effectively breaking their self-esteem and facilitating the surrender of information. The findings were never published. The sole recommendation was that any experiment of this nature would not be repeated.

Prologue

It was her white T-shirt that first drew my attention. It was late November and everyone else was wearing heavy jackets or coats. Yet this woman seemed oblivious to the cold wind.

She was about five yards away, fifteen feet of forecourt at a motorway service station. Her brown hair was pulled back in a ponytail, she wore black jeans and she had that stance, the stance of an athlete. The physical similarity was so great I couldn't help staring. The sun was on the horizon behind her and I was rooted to the spot, transfixed.

Could it be her? Really her?

I shook my head, trying to keep myself from acting stupidly and calling out. What was I thinking?

She'd finished filling up a white pickup, and as she walked to the kiosk she began stroking loose strands of her hair across her forehead – just the way Lima used to.

But it couldn't be Lima.

I wanted it to be, even though I knew it was impossible. It had been twenty years since I'd thought about her. There are some events in life that you need to keep locked away.

For me there were two; both involved Lima.

I had, as usual, driven to the gym after filling up at the service station. What wasn't normal was that I didn't remember any of that drive, and I didn't make it to the gym floor. I didn't make it outside the car. I just parked up and sat, hands on the steering wheel, looking out of the window. I wasn't just numb: time was standing still.

After a while a single thought slowly began to formulate in my mind. Eventually the thought formed a word. And that word found its voice.

'PESRE'.

I looked down at the ignition, took my right hand off the steering wheel and turned the key.

Twenty minutes later I pulled into the driveway of my house. Once inside I headed straight for the basement. It was not a place I visited very often. It was a relatively large room, about twenty feet square. It contained a vast quantity of containers and a number of the large boxes the British Armed Forces issued when you were posted overseas. Three of the MFO boxes, however, did not contain army kit: they contained files. Scores of them, thousands of sheets of paper. Millions of words.

The basement was my past.

I knew exactly what I was looking for, though I was afraid of finding it. I could see my hands trembling as I flicked through the file covers.

PESRE was a time when my world began to fall apart. Did I really need to find it? Too late now: I'd recognized the file. I stared at it for a full minute, trying to see its contents without opening it, aware that its beige cover was camouflage. I was looking at Pandora's Box.

My instincts screamed out that I should stop now, go back upstairs and forget about it. I knew the way to deal with this was to keep it locked up, and I'd done that. The file had remained effectively within arm's length but had been untouched for twenty years.

I sat down on the floor and drew a deep breath as I carefully opened the cover. The file contained transcripts of every conversation; and as for the things that hadn't been said – the feelings – they all came rushing back, as if a securely locked door had been broken open by a storm.

Day 1

August 1993

I leaned into the wind; it ripped and tugged at my coat as if determined to tear it apart. The rain battered against everything around me, the sound almost deafening. The guttering was unable to cope as rivers cascaded off rooftops. I was surrounded by waterfalls. I had my coat buttoned tight around my neck, but somehow the rain found its way down the back of my collar. I could feel my shirt, wet and cold, sticking to my back.

I was reporting to an army camp I hadn't even known existed, to take part in a secret military experiment. My brief was simple: to consult, and assist in the techniques used to extract information.

After the predictable delay at the guardroom I was escorted to the complex where the experiment was going to take place. It was on the west side of camp, and to get to it we crossed the parade ground, the stores, the NAAFI, the canteen, the gym and finally the officers' quarters, where I dropped off my bags. The complex was a relatively new build compared to the rest of the camp. In many ways it looked out of place; its steel-grey stone belonged in a sci-fi movie.

Roberts greeted me at the entrance. He was a hulking figure, a veritable giant, but his waistline was so enormous he was clearly not a soldier who trained for combat – if he was a soldier at all. That was the first thing about this that I didn't like: ranks and units were left outside the experiment, but, more noticeably, so were our real names. I didn't know who I would be working with; all I knew was that Roberts was in charge, and as for the rest, I wasn't to ask. All communication was to take place in the meeting room, which was where Roberts now led me, and where it all began...

'PESRE, gentlemen,' Roberts announced. 'Prolonged Extreme Stress Resistance Experiment. We are going to be identifying methods which will break a soldier who has proved resistant to interrogation techniques. We are going to experiment with a combination of techniques and identify the weak points in the subject; without breaking any international human rights legislation.'

'So we stay strictly within the confines of that legislation?'

I looked over at the short, stocky man who had asked the question. 'Smith' was the false name above his shirt pocket.

'We can bend it as far as we can without breaking it,' Roberts said, smiling.

I'd just met him and already I didn't like him. I'd never liked that phrase. If you used it, you had to define what 'breaking it' actually meant. In this case, probably that the information was to be extracted without the use of acknowledged methods of torture, which, according to the '84 UN Convention against Torture, was any act by which severe pain or suffering, whether physical or mental, is intentionally inflicted on a person for such purposes as obtaining from him, or a third person, information...

The goal, then, was to inflict stress and a level of pain and suffering, but nothing that would be interpreted as 'severe'. The breaking of morale would then be a cumulative effect. But the line that Roberts was intent on bending was far too fragile, and the use of the word 'extreme' in PESRE was contradictory and worrying.

From my experience whenever anyone said 'bend it as far we

can without breaking it' they really meant 'break the line as often as you want; just make sure you leave no evidence.'

'And what if the subject doesn't break?' Smith asked. 'We've done this kind of research before. It relies on the subject being motivated to withhold the information. The other problem is that the subject, who is, as I understand, a friendly, won't feel the level of fear a normal prisoner would, which makes findings inconclusive. We can't replicate interrogation conditions. The subjects always know we'll only go so far. And this is just one man; for any findings to be of at least some merit, shouldn't we be looking at a large group?'

'The key to this experiment is that it *is* only one subject: a volunteer who knows we're not going to hold back and has been ordered to withhold the information for as long as possible, and assist in the experiment by answering questions relating to techniques used. I have been assured that this subject is committed to withholding information.'

We hadn't even started and already I felt trapped.

Roberts continued. 'Currently, techniques that are deemed acceptable either don't obtain the information, or take too long. If you identify the way to break the most resilient, you have potentially found the quickest way to break everyone else.'

Or, it could end in the death of the subject and a full military inquiry.

I would have stood up and walked out of this right now. But the army isn't like that. In the army you take orders and get on with things. I would just have to make sure that if anything went wrong, I was covered.

'Is this exercise officially authorized?'

'I appreciate you asking this question, Johnson, and it's what I would expect from someone within this team. You and Smith were selected for your personal skills, but also for your integrity. This exercise is authorized at a very high level.'

Yeah, right. Authorized, but not officially.

'Gentlemen, it is crucial that we identify ways to obtain information from suspects as quickly as possible. This experiment will hopefully save lives. Now, there's no point in keeping this other information from you as you'll find out later today anyway, but the only thing we know is that the subject is a 26-year-old soldier, who was the best candidate. Do not let anything distract you, and remember this is not your ordinary soldier. This is a woman who has consistently performed at a higher level than all the men in her unit.'

'A woman? What is she, IDF?' I asked.

'It looks that way, and it's another reason why we shouldn't underestimate her. We all know how well trained the Israeli Defence Forces are, and if Lima's in one of their elite units, then we're going to have problems.'

Smith was clearly puzzled. 'Lima: I take it that's her call sign or code name. It's not a woman's name.'

'Lima was a Roman goddess,' I said quietly.

'Whatever. It's the name we've been given.' Roberts then rambled on about the Official Secrets Act before handing Smith and me a file which detailed our specific roles. It was full of the usual military terms, the usual bullshit, which overplayed the significance of the operation. Cut all that away and you were left with my main directives, and at least they made sense. I was to observe and regularly interview the subject to determine her mental fitness to continue, her motivation and the techniques she was applying to resist, and on completion (after the information had been extracted) compile a report establishing whether any techniques used to extract information, or to resist extraction, had viable applications; and make recommendations as to the direction of future tests.

Seeing it on paper made it seem almost feasible. But when the subject was a woman, there should have been at least one female on the team. Why the false names, and why only three of us? Roberts I didn't know about; Smith would be Medical, almost certainly a senior doctor, and I was Intelligence.

We were based in a section of the camp that was effectively isolated. We could draw on a select team of medical and support staff from the camp as required, but only if authorized by Roberts.

I somehow felt that aside from staff bringing in food it was going to be just the four of us. One woman whom we knew nothing about, but who had probably travelled around three thousand miles to be here, and three men committed to making her surrender a piece of worthless information.

I surmised that this was not just a clandestine operation where the emphasis was on concealment from the public, but a covert, or 'black' op, where the identity of the sponsor was also kept secret. The more I thought about it, the more apprehensive I became.

It didn't just have court martial written all over it. If the press got hold of it, it could mean an international inquiry into abuse by British military personnel.

It was a clusterfuck waiting to happen.

The first time I saw Lima was from the observation room. Her movements were measured and constrained, as if she was acclimatizing herself to the prison she now found herself in. Her brown hair was pulled back in a high, loose ponytail. Her physical presence was in her athleticism, particularly in the width of her shoulders. Yet for all that leverage and power there was a sense of intense femininity.

There was also something very familiar about her.

The first few days passed without much happening. These were observation days, Lima getting adjusted to her surroundings while we identified her normal physical and mental state before stress was applied.

She was kept isolated in the interview room. It was a big room by army standards, about thirty feet by twenty-five, with a toilet and shower off it. She'd been kitted out in standard issue combat boots, lightweight issue trousers, green General Service shirts and white T-shirts. She looked like an army recruitment poster girl.

Irrespective of what Roberts had told us, I couldn't see her lasting more than a few days before surrendering the information. Her physical conditioning wouldn't count for anything when we broke down her mind.

Yet odd things started happening even before the stress was applied. She was consuming a disproportionate amount of food, not just for a woman of her size but for a big man in basic training.

'She's taking in over eight thousand calories a day. What sort of medication is she on?' I asked Smith.

'From blood and urine samples, she's on no medication.'

This was the first sign of what we were dealing with. We had a video camera in the interview room linked up to VCRs and a TV monitor in the observation room, from where we watched her morning routine. She propped up the end of her bed, and with her feet off the raised end and hands on the floor, she worked her way through numerous sets of fifty incline press-ups. Her exercise routine also included one-legged squats: multiple compound sets with only a few seconds' rest in between. She refrained from sit-ups, or any form of aerobic activity, although the short time period between sets was clearly making her breathe heavily. For long periods throughout the day she lay on her bunk with her eyes closed.

'This isn't normal training. What's she up to?' Roberts asked.

I knew the answer but I let Smith explain it to him. 'Under conditions of stress, and particularly when food is denied, the body starts to eat off itself. It takes the best source of fuel available first – muscle – then fat. She's building muscle mass, and body weight in general.'

She was making herself as strong, and as heavy, as she could physically, and when she wasn't sleeping, preparing herself mentally.

She wasn't just IDF: she would be one of their best.

'Hey, down there! Two minutes!'

I'd been vaguely aware of Jacqueline getting in from work. I had sensed her moving around in the kitchen but it hadn't fully registered on my conscious until now. I made my way upstairs.

'It's a while since you were down there. Anything important?'

'I just have to check up on something, an exercise I was involved in years ago.'

I poured a glass of wine for Jacqueline, and helped her through with the dishes.

We were halfway through the meal before I remembered the similarity that had existed between my wife and Lima.

'You're not eating much,' Jacqueline said, then realized I was staring at her. 'What is it, what's wrong?'

I looked down at my plate. 'Nothing ... just tired, I guess. I'm not looking forward to hunting out information.'

'Why don't you have an early night and leave the work?'

'I'll see how it goes. I'll try and finish up in an hour.'

'One hour, really?'

One hour meant three at least. I made my way down the spiral staircase to the basement, tonight more than ever acutely aware of how much I missed the old Jacqueline. I had missed her for years.

We were living in the same house yet it felt like each of us was alone.

Lima was most definitely alone; fifteen days in, fifteen days with almost no sleep, the last three without food, the last two without water, sirens going off every five minutes. She was alone, without peace, without anything. She showed most of the typical symptoms that you would expect from lack of sleep: co-ordination off, listlessness, a general malaise.

But she gave nothing away. There was no fear, no distress, no sign of vulnerability. She had her steel front on, her armour; and for now it was impenetrable.

Although we'd been warned not to, we had underestimated her. We now realized that we were dealing with a soldier who was conditioned to adapt and improvise, in order to fight whatever was in front of her.

Day 17

Meeting Room

'I don't understand how she's coping,' Smith said. 'It's not just that she's been deprived of deep delta-wave sleep; she was being woken up as soon as she entered stage three deep sleep. When a sleep debt builds up, repeated disruption at the onset of deep sleep becomes increasingly traumatic. Somehow she was handling this, so I've gone for total sleep deprivation. Of course she's getting microsleeps without realizing it, but sleeps lasting less than thirty seconds won't make a significant difference. We've taken the stress levels to a point beyond anything I've ever experienced, yet she's not showing any indication of breaking.'

'The breaking point is there,' Roberts said flatly. 'We're just not hitting the right button. We have to make her feel fear.'

'If she's trained for combat that's not going to be easy,' I said.

Smith agreed. 'Soldiers who are combat-orientated typically see themselves as superior. We need to break her confidence.'

Roberts stared at me. 'You break confidence, you break the man. Johnson?'

'That would follow, yes.'

'But how do we break it?' Smith asked.

'Soldiers tend to rely heavily on their physical abilities. Let's get her body to betray her,' Roberts continued. 'Tell me, is not illness a symptom of self-betrayal?'

'Very much so,' Smith replied.

'Then we make her ill. I think it's a necessary course of action at this point.'

'How ill?'

'Let's take it in stages; it will be the deterioration that breaks her.'

'We are, in some ways, already making her ill,' Smith said. 'The immune system is hit hard by lack of sleep alone. It's only a matter of time before things start going wrong. She can't have much left in reserve.'

'We don't have time to wait. Let's induce illness.'

'Wait.' I blurted the word out. 'My understanding is that whatever we do is acceptable as long as it is not categorized as torture. Sleep deprivation, lack of food and water for periods, harassment: okay, maybe we can get away with that, but to make someone sick?'

'Everyone gets ill, Johnson,' Roberts announced, as if that was the end of the discussion.

'Yes, but they are not deliberately made ill.'

'Illness isn't torture,' retorted Roberts.

'I would be inclined to think anyone who has been seriously ill for a long period would describe it as torture,' Smith said. 'Prolonged physical pain and discomfort. It affects everything: eating, sleeping … It throws the body and mind into conflict. The stress and pressure is relentless. It erodes self-belief and self-worth, and in this sense it's absolutely perfect for destroying confidence. I can't imagine her withholding the information for more than a few days. In the long term it will be better for her. Hit her hard now, get the information, end this slow deterioration and restore her to health.'

Roberts smiled broadly. 'It's decided, then. What's the best way of doing this?'

Smith seemed just as enthusiastic. I guess he was thinking

of Lima's best interests. What he said about quickly ending the experiment made sense, though he had suspended medical ethics in the process.

'For what I have in mind, it'll be easy enough. We can give her an injection, or we can introduce it through food. The injection will be quicker.'

'Inject what?' I asked.

'That's not your area, Johnson.' Roberts turned to Smith. 'How long before it takes effect?'

'Approximately five hours, in her current state. She'll be struggling shortly after that.'

'Right, resume normal sleeping, eating and drinking today. How soon can you be ready?'

'Tomorrow morning.'

'Let her have a full day's break, lull her into a false sense of security, go in tomorrow night, hold her down and give her the injection.'

I concentrated, focusing on each word, ensuring I kept the anger out of my voice. 'Why hold her down? That's unnecessary.'

'We don't know that. Besides, I want this to be traumatic. We're trying to destroy her confidence, so let's start off by making her feel helpless; I want her to feel a victim.'

'I don't think it's a good idea.'

'Perhaps you could explain why?' The irritation was clear in Roberts's tone: he didn't like being questioned on the same subject more than once.

'She didn't volunteer for this.'

'She signed an agreement that stated we could do whatever we felt was necessary.'

'But did that agreement not also state that physical contact would be avoided?'

'Any contact made will be to ensure that a medical procedure takes place safely. This experiment has gone on long enough. We've been too gentle with her. Let's put an end to it. As Smith says, this will break any resistance she has left, and we can get her back to health again.'

He could word it any way he wanted, this was all about betrayal. This would make her feel a victim, and destroy her confidence. On the surface it would make the experiment more authentic, and give a better result, so, as Roberts saw it, the end would justify the means; but it didn't sit right with me. A contract had been made based on trust. Roberts was going to break that contract.

I was uneasy about something else. I would put money on it that Roberts and Smith had been pretending from the beginning that they didn't know each other. It also appeared that the medical and support staff had been hand-picked. This was Roberts's show.

Two questions wouldn't go away. What was I doing here? And how was Lima going to cope when her armour was stripped away?

In his wisdom, Roberts thought it would be a good idea for me to let her know that normal sleeping and eating would be restored. It would help add to the betrayal.

All the interviews were recorded. They picked up the slightest sound, so even whispering was out; but in training I'd learnt to lip-read. We didn't have any records on her; maybe *she* could? Although the video camera would be running, the interviews were regarded by Roberts and Smith as my area, and they allowed me to determine the positioning of the table and chairs. The camera was behind and above me but if Lima leant forward, anyone observing would get a good view of the room and my back, but not her.

Interview Room

Lima didn't acknowledge me sitting opposite her; she seemed lost, her eyes flashing in different directions – hallucinations, another side effect of sleep deprivation. She seemed to settle then and began absent-mindedly stroking loose strands of her hair across her forehead.

It was something that Jacqueline used to do. Despite the physical difference between them – Lima's athletic frame ideal for soldiering, Jaqueline waiflike and fragile – there were a number of similarities. I noticed the main one at the first interview – they both had the same extraordinary brown eyes. When the light caught them at a certain angle, they turned amber. Today, I found myself the focus of attention of those eyes, a focus so intense that, considering what we were going to do to her, I didn't know where to look. I also didn't know where to put my hands, so I rested them on the table.

At school a temp English teacher had just asked everyone in the class to give two sentences on how aspects of The Great Gatsby *related to their lives in 1970. Eilidh Anderson, who was never one to take anything seriously, stood up and with a big grin on her face announced, 'Buchanan has a body capable of great leverage; a cruel body.' First sentence gone. 'He,' pointing towards me in accusation, 'he has Buchanan's hands.'*

The teacher protested at first but her voice faded into an embarrassing silence when she turned and looked at them. I had always been conscious of my hands, because what my classmate had said was true: they were enormous. I was always breaking things, pulling door handles off by accident. For my fifteenth birthday my mother had given up trying to buy gloves to fit me, and knitted them instead.

I hadn't felt this conscious of them since that day. I enveloped my left hand in my right as I used to do then, convincing myself this would make them look smaller. I started off just as Roberts would expect. 'Do you want to give me the information?'

'No.'

'They're going to restore water, food and sleep. Things will be normal.' I mouthed the next words, exaggerating the lip movements ... *They are going to break the conditions of the experiment. Lean forwards, out of the camera's line of sight* ... 'For a while, anyway.'

She stared at me.

Trust me ... please.

'I will be allowed to sleep?' She leant slowly forwards on her elbows.

'You're being given the opportunity to restore your strength.' *Be careful.*

'Did you recommend this?' she asked. Her lips then moved in silence. *Of what?*

'No, the medical officer.' *Something will happen tomorrow night.*

'I feel okay.' *What?*

'Well, we have protocol to follow.' *An injection. They're going to make you ill. Be ready.*

'When am I going to get water and food?'

'As soon as we finish here.'

She stood up and moved away from the table.

'Then we are finished.'

I stood up and began pacing about the basement. I couldn't handle the feelings of helplessness then and I couldn't handle them now. My throat was dry. I climbed the spiral staircase for a glass of water. When I was leaving the kitchen, I walked past the stairs. The hall lights were off but there was a soft glow coming from the bedroom.

Jacqueline had taken to leaving the bedside light on all night now. I knew she was having nightmares, though she wouldn't talk about them. She was like a child, lost in the dark. She had been lost for years, and I had felt helpless throughout. I wanted to go upstairs and try to comfort her. I *had* tried, so many times, but I'd tried when it was too late.

The moment I sat down with the file in my hands, I was transported back to camp.

Despite the fact that I had established a secret line of communication with Lima, I was distraught. The night of the injection I stayed in my quarters. I couldn't face seeing what they were going to do to her, yet I kept imagining what was going on. A select team of the strongest men Roberts could get hold of, charging into the interview room with Smith sauntering in behind them holding a syringe ... Lima, defiant, resisting, fighting, but being overwhelmed in her weakened state by sheer force of numbers, her arms and legs held, her feet lifted off the ground, pulled onto her bunk, hands all over her, men holding her down...

The images tormented me the whole night.

I turned up early the next morning. They told me there had been no resistance; that it all went smoothly. They had gone in just as Roberts had planned, gently restrained her and injected her with some kind of infection. I didn't believe them. I couldn't see Lima not resisting – she may have volunteered for this, and she may have signed a piece of paper allowing anything to be done to assist in the experiment, but there was supposed to be no physical contact. How much more physical could you get?

Lima lay on her bunk all that day, and the next three days. She vomited throughout each of those days and her temperature was running high. Nursing and medical staff were brought in to treat her under Smith's supervision. There was minimum communication with her; she was treated just as if she was a terror suspect.

I had done what I could to prepare her for this, but deep down I knew I should have been able to stop it from happening. She wouldn't communicate with me, other than telling me she wasn't going to surrender the information. She announced this the moment I stepped into the interview room. Even when I knew it was coming, it still felt like a backhand slap across my face, and I would immediately step back out again.

Over the following days, the fever and vomiting subsided somewhat. When it came, it came in waves. Most of the time her condition was classed as stable, but it was clear that for long periods she was in distress. She'd stopped exercising, and she was barely eating. Then, on Day 26, it happened. She got up, went for a shower (something she hadn't done for days), dressed, forced herself to eat breakfast, then turned the wooden table over, prised off one of its thick legs and, using it like a club, systematically began destroying the interview room. The mirrors went first. She smashed them all. The lights went next, then she broke up the two chairs used for the interviews. With the exception of her bunk, her clothes locker and, interestingly, the video camera, she destroyed everything.

Two of the camp's Regimental Police went in to restrain her. They were big men, around my size, men used to violence; and seeing them advance on a much smaller and ill woman I was on the point of running through to stop them. But just as I was shifting my weight to start my run, Lima casually tossed away the table leg. The action was totally unexpected, and confusing. Her stance, and the indifference with which she discarded the table leg, were not indicative of someone about to surrender; rather, someone preparing for conflict. But as a soldier you are trained to fight using whatever weapons are available – unless, of course, your bare hands are more effective. Hypnotized by the monitor screen I stood immobile, transfixed, watching as the destruction unfolded.

If you had to describe in one word the close-combat fighting art developed in Israel for use by the IDF it would be 'effective'. Krav Maga, Hebrew for contact combat, was conceived in the mid '30s by Imi Lichtenfeld, then developed and refined by him over several decades. It has a philosophy emphasizing threat neutral-ization, simultaneous defensive and offensive manoeuvres, and aggression. I'd seen it demonstrated a few years before and was stunned by just how effective it was. However, the soldier who had disarmed and neutralized four men in less than ten seconds was, I now realized, using a form of the art which had been adapted for demonstrations. As I watched Lima in action there was really only one word you could use to describe Krav Maga: 'brutal'.

They sent in a team of medics to pull the RPs out. One had a broken arm, the other a broken wrist, dislocated shoulder and, we were informed later by the hospital, a ruptured testicle, which had to be removed.

Roberts was raging. I told him we were lucky she hadn't killed them. Which we were. Lima was probably an advanced instructor. I took it that she was giving us a warning: do not get physical with me again.

After that things slowly returned to as normal as they could be. She allowed the lights to be replaced, and the table and chairs; but not the mirrors. It was deemed an acceptable compromise. She began exercising again, although this only entailed walking around the room, and my interviews with her resumed.

Lima's speech was strained and broken. She became tired and we often had to take long breaks, giving her time to lie down and rest. I frequently had to ask the same question several times before I could accurately establish her answer. The transcripts I typed from recordings were adjusted accordingly. At times I used my own words to join up her broken speech.

Day 30

Interview Room

Lima appeared physically weak, and was running a temperature.

'The information?'

She shook her head.

'Why don't you stop this?'

Silence.

'Stop this pain and discomfort, get your health back and start living again.'

'That would mean disobeying orders.'

'Your orders are to withhold the information, but only for as long as you can.'

'Evidently I can still withhold.'

'It's only going to get worse. There's nothing to prove; you've gone further than anyone else.'

'You think I'm trying to prove something?'

'I'm not sure what to think any more.' *I'm not happy with what's happening.*

'The weather?' *What is happening?*

You're being used. 'What?'

'What's it like outside?' *Am I? You do not know why I am here.*

'Why don't you give me the information and you can find out for yourself?' *Why are you here?*

'It is not so important.' *I chose to be here. I need to be here.*

Why? 'How are you coping? How are you handling the pain?'

That's irrelevant. 'Pain? You should know this.'

'I know that all pain originates in the brain,' I said.

'That means nothing by itself. You have to break it down to understand it.'

'What's to understand? Even if you did understand, it doesn't mean you can control it.'

She looked right through me.

'Okay, Lima, if you've found a way to understand and control pain, then I ... we, are all interested; that's why we're here.' *Is this a way out of something?*

There never was a way out. 'Pain is all about perception. If you are concerned that the pain is the result of damage, then you focus on it as a warning signal and it is exaggerated in your mind as a result. The opposite is true for an athlete running up a hill. He feels the increasing pain in his legs due to lactic acid build-up. He knows what the pain is and he knows the more of this pain he endures the stronger he will become.'

'I understand that, Lima, but perception can only go so far, and the athlete running up the hill knows the pain will be short-lived. Research has shown that when you know when pain will end it is far easier to bear.'

'That's irrelevant. The key is your perception – what you focus on. If you can shut down the body's warning system you can do what you want with the pain. Top athletes recondition their brains to love one aspect of the pain, the part that is making them stronger. Recondition yourself to love your ability to endure it. Recognize the part of it that can't break you, acknowledge that and what do you get?'

I shrugged my shoulders.

'Confidence; confidence in yourself that encourages you to

think you can do things that you have never done before. The fact that you confront and endure pain without fear gives you this confidence. That is the positive part of it; you focus on that, you love that. You complicate when it is really simple. The more pain I endure, the greater my confidence. That is all the pain is to me now; confidence is something I need, it is crucial to any task.'

It was extreme though I could see the logic in it, but only if confidence was that important to you.

As I was leaving the interview room I turned to look at Lima. There was something different from the last interview two weeks ago. She'd clearly lost weight but something was missing. Later I realized it was the green and black cord for her diskit, the IDF-issue one-piece version of dog tags. I hadn't noticed when watching from the monitor. She could have stopped wearing it anytime in that fortnight, though it was more probable that it had been torn off when they introduced the illness.

I switched my mind onto something else. It would be too traumatic to go there again.

That evening I phoned Jacqueline. She wasn't in. I was disappointed: I had wanted to hear her voice. I hated being away from her for any length of time.

December 1976. The snow had stopped falling but it would be another day before the roads were clear. A Land Rover with four-wheel drive would make it, but not my car. I was due at her place at noon, and we were to spend the day together before I went back on duty at ten that night. I called to tell her I'd be a few hours late, then walked fifteen miles across country. I only had half an hour with her before I had to start back and I made no advances to her during that time. We just sat and talked, and then hugged and I left. I would smile whenever she said I was crazy to have walked that distance when we could have talked on the phone. I knew she loved it, though; she loved the way I made her feel special, the little things, like the way I refused to abbreviate her name.

A year later we married. They say that after the first couple of years of marriage the passion fades; with Jacqueline that didn't happen. When we'd been apart, even for a day, when we met she always took my breath away. There was a part of me that just needed to see her. It didn't seem possible that I would ever take what I'd walked thirty miles for – to see her face – for granted.

Back at my quarters I changed into my green lightweight trousers, laced up my boots and threw on a sweatshirt. It was a warm evening, so I didn't bother warming up. I started out at a jog and within a few minutes I was running at a good pace. After so many years in the army I had reached a level of fitness where running becomes an act of freedom as opposed to exercise. The faster I ran, the more of Roberts' and Smith's hypocrisy I left behind.

I hadn't planned my route and found myself running along the side of a wood. I ran mostly in the shadow of the trees but every few seconds the sun glinted through and for a brief moment I would bathe in flashes of warm light. This was a wood that had existed for centuries and with there being no pattern to the breaks in the trees it felt as if the sun was talking to me in Morse code. I ran faster, reading the letters and words in my mind.

It was to be a brief spell of freedom.

In between the words came images of Lima bent over, vomiting...

I accelerated, running as far away as I could get from the observation room. I was out of the trees and had found my way into another army camp. This one hadn't been occupied by troops for years. There were rows of adjoining houses: married quarters, homes supplied to soldiers to house them, their wives and families for the length of their posting. Long, curved lines of houses, row upon row, crescents from the past. They resembled the old mining towns from the '30s and '40s. Then they would have bustled with life, but now empty they were part of a ghost town.

What was odd about them was their size. There was a narrow door, a small window alongside it, then the doorway of the next house. There was no gap between them, no room to breathe.

The sun was out of sight behind them and the image of Lima vomiting was interspersed with a more torrid image. The question I'd shut out earlier burst through. They'd ripped her diskit off, but Smith wouldn't want clothing to get in the way of the injection and, with Roberts wanting this to be as traumatic as possible for Lima, I was certain that the men he had used had torn off whatever she'd been wearing.

I was blazing along the crescent now, trapped in the claustrophobia of these tiny houses and the images of Lima, stripped, struggling against a number of men, a rape of trust taking place while I paced around my quarters, doing nothing.

My sprint ended at the point where the houses finished and opened out onto clear ground. I doubled over, tried to stand with my hands on my knees, but I sank to the ground, curling into a ball, my stomach going into convulsions, vomit jetting out of my mouth. I gasped for breath as sweat broke out over my whole body. I lay still for a long time after my stomach had emptied, getting to my feet only when my breathing returned to normal.

The images didn't return as I expected, probably because I was caught up in the scene in front of me. I sat down on a low wall and watched the sun set on the horizon. Some way off was a rectangle – a hundred by eighty feet, containing the set of metal obstacles, now rusting, around six feet high, which you had to clamber over to get to the twelve-foot wall, the ditch that would have been full of muddy water, the scramble net for men to roll over, the wooden beams for men to run across, the long ropes suspended for them to climb.

I could hear the voices echoing from my past, the screams of the physical training instructors, ordering, pushing, demanding ... I watched the shadows come to life on the assault course, the dreaded assault course, the loathed assault course. The place of basic training where recruits were initiated into army life and tested to breaking point; the place of punishment and sweat and vomit and torn muscle and ruptured ligaments.

How many soldiers had gone across this course? How many had been toughened and hardened by it? The assault course did that to you: it pushed you to the limit, it made you realize that there was a point in you that you could go beyond; there was hidden potential, and it wrenched some of that potential out of you.

The great irony of it was that all those soldiers who had crossed this one would have been men, and almost all of those men would, like me, have hated it.

Lima would have loved it.

As the sun disappeared behind the hill, casting a purple shadow over the course, I saw her approaching. Her arms loose at her side, her step light, her head arched back ever so slightly, her face and neck bathed in the evening light.

I had found a place of sanctuary. I sat on the low wall, picturing Lima, the wind sweeping her hair back, running free, smiling as she clambered across the metal framework, rolling over the scramble net, hurling herself around this course. It would have been a playground for her, because the assault course was pain. Lima believed she understood pain, and that belief allowed her to use it.

Yet there was much more to Lima than merely the ability to tolerate and use pain. Her world was driven by something I was still trying to understand. It was as if there were no limits to what she could do.

Day 35

Interview Room

There had been a lot of mouthing and lip-reading today; much of the conversation had taken place in silence. I had been expressing concern about the high risk of getting caught up in using pain and missing the bigger picture: the permanent damage that was taking place. Then suddenly without warning Lima had ended the silent conversation and it was all out in the open.

'This is about a principle,' she said firmly. 'Rules apply here.'

'Rules?'

'There are two fundamental rules that apply to any important task or challenge. Rule One: before you begin a task you must first succeed in your mind. Rule Two: you have to make what you are doing, i.e. the task, more important than your life. You would rather die than fail.'

I was struggling to take this in. I was caught off balance by the sheer severity of Rule Two. 'Okay. What, in your situation, do you deem as succeeding?'

'Withholding the information.'

'And what about your deteriorating condition?'

'My mission is to withhold the information; everything else is secondary. To complete the mission all I have to do is endure, nothing else. I know I can do that; it's not an issue. Yet I want, and need, to fight the illness. There is a power to belief, I know there is; so I do what I can to truly believe in recovery. I pretend, I force myself to play out films of the future. If I cannot do that then I flash images of the future.'

'What future?'

'The future I want.'

'Believing in recovery may help some medical conditions, but you don't know what's wrong.'

'What is my condition, then? What was that crap they put into me?'

'I don't know.' *I don't know. They won't tell me.*

'So it is an unknown. I cannot find out, so there is no point in making an assumption that belief will not work. It might work. That is all I need to know: the odds of it working or not working are irrelevant. It is the principle that matters. I do what I can ... all I can. And that means believing. What else is there?'

'There's always something else.'

'You are wrong. You are just like everyone else who wants to think there is something else, because believing on its own is against intellect. You cannot handle the idea of making belief your primary purpose in life. You feel there must be something tangible you can do, or at the very least some proof that belief works. So you search for evidence, you search for signs; and if you find them you look for more, just to be sure. You will never have enough proof; you will never have enough to feel safe.'

'Safe from what?'

'Despair. The despair that will hit you if you lose the belief. Believing in the future you want has a cost – it sets you up for despair. The more you believe, the worse the potential despair. You are afraid to believe.'

'But you're not?'

'If I was I would be unable to fight effectively. I will only despair if I lose the belief. But if I persevere and keep fighting, I will not lose anything.'

'What if you can't persevere?'

'Why should I stop?'

'It's a natural reaction, to doubt, isn't it?'

'Not if you believe in yourself.'

'That takes a hell of a lot of self-belief, Lima.'

'Why do you complicate everything? The only way I can fight is by striving to believe. I fight or I do not. I persevere, or I do not. There is no in-between.'

'You believe, or you don't?'

'You can only believe when you have self-belief. Without that confidence you will not take risks: you will be too afraid of despair. With it, you become indifferent to risks. The ability to believe and self-belief are almost inseparable.'

For Lima, believing was all about creating another reality, relentlessly programming it until you reached the point where your mind was effectively tricked into accepting it. It was an art frequently used by magicians: misdirection – what the eyes see and the ears hear, the mind believes. Lima was using everything she could to substitute present with future, substituting the bleak negatives of today's reality for the positives of a dream future. I had thought there would be more, but it was all about hard work, staying on course and persevering in the face of negative feedback. I had hoped to find a flaw in her logic which I could use to convince her to surrender the information. But the obstacle would always be Rule Two – if completing her mission of withholding the information was more important than her life, it wouldn't matter what flaws appeared.

That evening I found I couldn't go out for my run. As it transpired I was never to visit the assault course again. I couldn't face enjoying the sights and sounds of an autumn evening while Lima was locked away in that room.

It was 0200 and I was wide awake. I had thought I was beginning to understand Lima, then from nowhere she had introduced two rules that were stunning in their simplicity. But why bring something as dangerous as Rule Two into play? The reason she would go to such extremes eluded me. Lima was caught up in a strategy that in shutting out feedback was straying further and further away from reality. To what end? Where would it lead her? And where did her rules originate?

I walked over to the observation room. The soldier on guard passed me through. I sat down and watched the monitor screen. I thought Lima would be lying asleep but she was up and walking slowly around the edge of the room. She was walking circuits; this was her training, her physiotherapy. She was preventing the muscles from atrophying completely. But it was obvious this was a trial for her. After each lap she stopped, leaned against the wall for a few seconds, and then began another lap.

Then she fell. She got up and fell again. She worked her way onto one knee, and leaning on the knee she hauled herself up, then steadied herself and took one step forward. She fell before she made the second step.

She took longer this time to work her way onto one knee. With a scream she wrenched herself upright. Then, supporting herself against the wall with one hand, she vomited. Afterwards she slid down the wall to the floor, and sat there panting.

I knew medical staff would appear at any second. They would

be watching the same scene on another monitor in another building. Sure enough they appeared. One male, one female. Each went either side of Lima to help her up. She brushed them off and worked her way up onto one knee; but this time as she stood up she blacked out. The nurses caught her before she hit the ground. They lifted her back onto the bed, waiting with her until she regained consciousness.

It had been a mistake coming here tonight. I was trembling as I walked back to my quarters. I took no consolation in the knowledge that Lima was receiving a good level of care when she was in danger. All we were doing was keeping her alive; we weren't doing anything to stop the progress of whatever Smith had injected into her.

That was being left to run its course.

Day 41

I don't know how many press-ups I was on now: I'd lost count at a hundred. Yet I kept pressing until my arms gave out and I slumped to the floor, my head to the side, gulping in breaths of air, too exhausted to notice the burning in my arms and shoulders.

I stepped out of my quarters. The air was fresh and light. It was one in the morning and most of the camp was asleep. It was a cloudless night. As I walked across the parade ground, I realized that any attempts to expel destructive emotions would fail. Lima was still in that room and any time I spent pushing my body was just a momentary distraction.

The moon cast my shadow in front of me; after the press-ups my shoulders seemed enormous, but I could feel them buckling under the weight of oppression. I wandered around for a while, then found myself at our complex. The guard on the door recognized me and saluted.

I went into the observation room. The video recorders were still whirring along. I sat and looked at the monitor screen. Lima was lying on her bunk, asleep.

I'd lost track of time; I didn't know how long had passed but Lima was sitting up on the edge of her bed. What was she doing? Was it just restlessness? She lay back down on the bed. Two minutes later she was sitting up again, this time vomiting into a sick bowl. She was retching every few seconds, but as the minutes passed it was clear something was very wrong: this was going on too long.

I quickly walked to the entrance to the interview room.

The guard had left his post. The place seemed deserted.

Lima was coughing over the sick bowl when I went through the door. Her body was trembling, her hair was wet and sticking to her forehead, her T-shirt, soaked, was hanging off her now thin frame. She looked at me, and screamed.

'Go away! GO AWAY!'

I burst outside, running. I started towards the assault course, but it wouldn't be far enough. I wanted to be miles away from here. I wanted to be in another world, where there were no wars or torture, or illness, or experiments.

When I stopped running I was at Roberts's quarters. I didn't know how I'd ended up here.

There would be a patrol but I figured they would be in another area of the camp. I slipped into his room through an open window. He was snoring loudly. I stood over him and watched. After a few minutes his snoring became unbearable. I gently wrapped my fingers around his throat. The snoring stopped. I could feel the roughness of his skin. His neck, though thick, felt tiny in my hands. He stirred, his eyes slowly opening. I tightened my grip. His eyes widened. He tried to lift his head up, but I pressed down harder. He tried to wrench his body out of bed, but I was kneeling on his chest. He tried to speak but there was silence save for the whisper of the wind from outside the window. His eyes were bulging now as his body started to go into convulsions. My grip tightened, squeezing, crushing, tearing...

I slipped out of the window. With luck I would be out of the camp and at the airport long before Roberts was discovered.

Lima!

I ran to the complex. The guard was still missing. I ran straight in and over to her bunk. She was asleep. I cradled her in my arms and, with the blankets wrapped around her, lifted her up.

We were outside and I was running towards the car park. Lima weighed so little I carried her easily. She stirred, looked up at me, and smiled.

'Not far now,' I whispered to her. But my heart sank as I noticed a line of soldiers one hundred yards ahead, blocking my path. The car park was blocked off.

I turned and another line of soldiers were there, and advancing. I looked around and all I could see were lines of soldiers, shining flashlights, slowly advancing towards us.

There was no way out.

I could feel her hand gently grip my forearm. I looked at her again.

'There is always a way. You will find it,' she said.

But where?

'You will find it.' Her words were calming; she had total confidence in me. She was that certain.

I heard a loud thud, followed by an even louder one. As I opened my eyes I felt a rush of adrenaline. I lifted my head up from the desk. On the monitor screen I saw Lima pick one of the chairs up off the floor. She began to walk laboriously around the room using the chair as a walking-frame.

How long had she been at this? How long had I been asleep?

I rubbed my eyes, running my fingers down my face. There had been a pattern to my dreams recently, always ending in a similar manner. I focused on the monitor in an attempt to dispel the images from the dream.

Lima's progress was painfully slow. After five turns around the room she lay down on her bed, then slowly pulled the covers over herself. She was lying on her back, facing the camera, her eyes open. She was looking at me without realizing it.

I watched her for an hour, wondering what images she was projecting from the future. Her eyelids began flickering, then closed.

What did she dream of when she was unable to exert a level of control? Was it the future she desired, or the monsters from the present?

Day 43

There is a way. You will find it.

Even though they had only been said in a dream, the words stayed with me. I lay in bed looking up at the ceiling. There was no way out for Lima. The prolonged stress must be affecting her. I hadn't really considered insanity as being the outcome. But who was going insane? Out of the four personnel on PESRE, Lima would be the obvious choice; but there were times when it seemed she was the only one of us thinking clearly.

I looked at my watch: 0430. I knew I wouldn't get back to sleep now. I stood up and looked out of the window, recalling the conversation from the previous day.

'The rules, Lima: were they part of your training?'

'I took them from a book.'

I asked her if it was a self-help book and she laughed. It was the first time I'd seen her smile this way. It lit up her whole face and with it my world because in those seconds all the deceit and hypocrisy of PESRE was insignificant.

'Ever heard of Joe Greenstein?' she asked.

I shook my head.

'He was a strongman who grew up in Poland at the turn of the century before emigrating to the States. There he began practising feats of strength that defied logic. He carried on performing these feats into his eighties. He had learnt how to tap into a higher power. He used his mind to do things no one else could do. When

I read his biography I noticed that two principles kept coming up. These principles form the two rules.'

Lima went on to tell me more about this man, and as she spoke my world that her smile had lit up began to fade. I looked closer at her face; her cheekbones that at the beginning of the experiment had a lovely softness to them were now harsh and angular, her beautiful brown eyes that burned amber ... dark shadows underneath them. I was more afraid than ever for her now. It seemed the foundations for all her strategies came directly from a book about a man who supposedly held back aeroplanes with his hair, and bent iron bars using his mind.

As I left the interview I felt a deep sadness. She was so convinced; she truly believed in these rules. Where would they take her? How many stories did I know about people who went with belief instead of medication? Almost every story ended tragically. If only Lima had the benefit of both.

I looked at Rule Two purely as a point of logic. You would have to make not just a life-changing but a life-determining decision before applying it. The rule meant that you committed yourself to one course of action, one future; and once the rule was set, that future then held you in its grasp until it was attained ... or you died.

What sort of life would you have if the future you chose was impossible?

I couldn't think this way; I was writing off her strategy because what it was based on was too fantastic.

I decided to ignore yesterday's conversation. I would pretend it hadn't happened.

I asked myself the question that had been troubling me from the onset: why had she volunteered for this experiment? Was it simply her frustration with the system? Prior to the formation of the IDF in 1948 women were actively involved in combat;

thirty-three women of the Palmach, the elite fighting force, were killed during the Israeli War of Independence. But after that war, although women still trained for combat they were taken off front-line combat duty. There were a number of reasons given for this, one being that their male counterparts began to behave unpredictably in battle when the women in their unit were wounded or at risk of being captured. The primordial need to protect overrode their training. I felt that if women had been allowed combat duty Lima would have joined the Sayeret Matkal, the IDF's Special Forces unit which was modelled on the SAS and had adopted their motto – Who Dares Wins: it had her written all over it.

Things would change, but in 1993 perhaps the only way women in the IDF could fulfill a deep need to fight was by volunteering for military experiments like PESRE. But why would she have such a great need to fight? Lima continued to confuse me. It was as if she had adopted her own motto acknowledging the power of belief. Who dares to dream, and perseveres, wins.

But at what cost?

Day 45

Another pointless meeting with Roberts and Smith had just ended. I walked back to my quarters. The sun, hidden behind clouds, broke out and for a few minutes bathed the sky in dark orange.

She was missing all of this, alone in that room, isolated and in pain. She was missing all the things I took for granted, like seeing the sky, like feeling the wind brush against my face. You put a soldier in a cage, and I think that's the thing they'll miss most. Sure, they'll miss their loved ones, they'll miss the family within their unit, but at a deep level they'll miss being close to nature.

Lima must be missing it: she frequently asked about the weather outside. Yet I'd persuaded Roberts into allowing her outside for a short time every other day – no strings attached. She'd turned the offer down. From what she said about it, she seemed to have found a way of not just enduring hardships, but using them to give her confidence that she would attain her goal. She appeared to be putting off anything that could be deemed pleasurable until after the experiment was over. I could see it might make her feel that she was exerting a level of control, and it would give her something to visualize: a symbol, a reward in the future. Everything, however, was dependent on her attaining her goal. She was committing herself to, and risking everything on, this future, a future that was all in her mind and might never happen.

I walked over to the complex.

Interview Room

'When I was prevented from sleeping, all I felt was an overpowering desire to sleep. A part of me wanted to die, because then I would sleep. You become numb to everything except that. It is not so much the physical, it's the mental strain, a constant pressure, and your mind can only function on one level, focus on one thing. It's unable to handle anything more. Nothing makes sense; you just stop caring.'

'But you still refused to surrender the information,' I said. 'You would have been allowed to sleep if you had. So why didn't you? This is important, Lima; this is the information we're looking for.'

'No it is not. Everyone has their own reason for doing something; it is personal to them. Sometimes it is real, sometimes it is imagined; but it gives them justification. They use logic to justify. You do not want the reason, you want the how.'

She was wrong: for the experiment I may have wanted the how, but I was far more interested in the why. I wanted to understand the woman. I wanted to know what drove her.

'Imagine you suddenly find yourself on a barren planet in the furthest reaches of the galaxy.'

'Okay,' I said, unsure of where this was going.

'And you know there is no one else on this planet, and it is just flat ground. There is only the light from the other stars. You breathe normally, but you have no need of food or water. And you know that no one, nothing, will ever come within light years of this planet. You are completely alone. You know what my question is?'

'Can I stay sane?'

'No. How *long* do you think you can stay sane? It is just a question of time, of hours, minutes, maybe even seconds. You have no need to do anything, so you have no need for logic and no framework to attach it to. It is not like going back to ancient times: then, there was always survival; now, you do not have to eat, or sleep. You have nothing as a starting or finishing point. You have no direction whatsoever. It is as if one second stretches into eternity, and for the duration you are alone.'

'But then you are effectively dead.'

'You can't think if you're dead. But you can think on this planet. You can think without the limitations of logic, without the clutter of life.'

'Pure thought,' I said.

'I suppose you could call it that.'

'So that's where you went to when you couldn't function without sleep?'

'No, that is where I went to find a reason, a way to keep going. You cannot escape from that kind of pressure without sleep, with sirens going off all the time. It is just about finding a reason to endure it.'

'I don't understand.'

'The how came from a place without logic, so I cannot explain it to you. All I can do is show you the place where I found it.'

I was lost; I wasn't sure if she was providing genuine information to help the experiment, if she was trying to confuse me, or if her physical deterioration was dramatically affecting her thought process.

I changed the subject. 'Lima: that's not your real name, is it?'

'No, but very close.'

I tried to guess her name that day, and in the days ahead, but every time I tried she would smile and shake her head. It was just a game to her. I kept trying. I went through every Jewish and Western name beginning with Li, but I never got it right. I never found out if it would be a way to reach out to the child in her, and bring an end to this madness.

Down in the basement twenty years later I skimmed through the next days in the file. They were the same: a slow, gradual deterioration physically, contrasting with a strengthening resolve to withhold the information. Lima had a set course, and was driving towards her target. Her body was a battlefield, her mind at war; yet somehow she was on the offensive.

Day 52

It had been a long day. After my meeting with Lima, I took a shower and lay on my bunk exhausted. I shut my eyes but I could not shut out the ever-growing desire to find an escape route for her. Today, finally, I had been given answers to the question that had been baffling Smith and Roberts: how had she remained in control on a day-to-day, hour-to-hour basis?

You put Lima's strategies together and they were far more than the sum of their parts. They interlinked to create a very extreme form of mental combat. Lima called it Krav Nafshi. One of the fundamental aspects was the way the mind used what would ordinarily be seen as negative and destructive. Using it, Lima would search out something in the negative that either built confidence or increased drive and when she found it she would focus only on that. All the negatives associated with it were endured to obtain the one positive.

Of course it was a selective approach to life, but how far would Lima take the principle? Would she deliberately damage something she cared about, and link her erasing the damage, making amends, to an event she would take part in after she had succeeded in her mission? Or would she take it to the furthest extreme, where she would sabotage everything she cared about in the present, leaving only the opportunity for redemption in the future?

I was asking myself questions but I already knew the answers.

Lima wasn't just creating shame and using it as fuel. Once she'd sabotaged everything important in her life she would have nothing left to lose. This made the application of Rule Two viable. Lima was, by her actions, making the attainment of her goal more important than her life – she *would* rather die than fail.

Yes, that was it: she would use this mental combat to enforce Rule Two. At that moment, I knew not just the military term for Krav Nafshi but also precisely how all this was going to end. I looked at my watch: it was just after eight. I dressed in a white shirt, my Corps tie and a navy suit, grabbed a bottle of wine I'd been saving for my next leave and made my way over to the senior officers' married quarters on the other side of camp.

I was certain Roberts would have been given accommodation here. The houses were more like mansions, the polar opposite of the rabbit hutches I'd passed on my run.

I was in luck: two soldiers on camp guard were patrolling nearby. I called to them and approached at a fast walk, then told them in my best impersonation of an Old Etonian that I was 'frightfully late for a dinner party. I'm not sure which house it is. Roberts, great big chap, about six ten.'

They bought it; they didn't know his name but they knew exactly who I was referring to.

Three minutes later I was standing on his porch. When I rang the bell it was Roberts himself who opened the door.

'How did you find ... how did you get through the guard? Never mind; what are you doing here, Johnson? You know damn well communication outside of meetings isn't permitted.'

'I appreciate that, but this won't wait.'

He looked from me to his watch, and sighed. 'You have two minutes.'

'I think we need to end the experiment tonight. Lima's strategy is making it impossible for her to surrender the information. She's found a way of using adversity.'

'She'll break, don't worry about it; she'll surrender the information.'

'She's turned it into Total War.'

'Total War? Johnson, you've become too close to this. Total War, really? As soon as she gives over the information I'll recommend that you have an extended period of leave. You're not sleeping, are you?'

'I don't think you understand what we're dealing with.'

'I know exactly: a soldier who is physically and mentally exhausted and has gone way beyond the time we expected. She now has no reason to withhold the information.'

'Aside from her obeying orders. She was ordered to withhold the information,' I said, aware I was beginning to sound like Lima.

'Only for as long as possible.'

'But that's the thing with the most professional soldiers. They obey orders – you tell them to run up a hill, they run until they reach the top, or their legs collapse underneath them, or they pass out. They go on until the body fails. She's going to do just that, but it won't be her legs failing. She has never even considered surrendering the information, and she won't.'

Roberts smiled. 'The pain and discomfort is wearing her down; it's just a matter of days now.'

'But pain is just fuel for her; she's thriving off it. Her strategy is allowing her to use everything we throw at her. This is where this experiment has a fundamental problem because the more pressure we apply the stronger she's becoming mentally.'

'Even though she's becoming weaker physically? That's in direct opposition to human nature. I've never even heard of that before. That's absurd.' Roberts looked down and laughed silently.

I could feel the adrenaline begin to flow.

'Johnson, your two minutes are up. It doesn't matter what her strategy is, she'll still break.' He took a step backwards.

'You're missing the point: she *can't* break.'

I was talking to a closed door.

Observation room

I watched Lima on the monitor. She was restless this evening, throwing the covers off, then wrapping herself up in them. Her monsters were out in force tonight.

'She can't break.' The words had just come out, but now I was certain my instincts were right. The change in her didn't happen at the moment of the betrayal of trust with the injection, nor in the days immediately after it when she was violently ill. It took place later when her condition showed a steady and relentless deterioration. Then Lima would have realized that what had been injected into her was going to keep eating away inside her until she surrendered the information. That was the point when the full extent of the betrayal had surfaced. She would have been angry at putting her trust in a team of men she didn't know. Destroying the interview room was, I now believed, a ploy to get men to try to overpower her while she still had some strength left. There was an ease to the move which broke the first RP's arm, but it was the second and bigger RP who she really worked over. The level of brutality she displayed made me wonder if he had been in the team who went in with Smith the night of the injection. She disabled him quickly so there was no need for more violence, but when she had him on the ground, holding his arm extended, she snapped his wrist as she stamped her heel on his groin; then, after lifting her foot, stamped again, this time on his shoulder while simultane-ously wrenching his arm.

It was systematic, methodical and emotionless.

The RP was currently still in the army, but that was a mere technicality. He would be discharged in the coming weeks on medical grounds: according to the full report almost every tendon in his right shoulder had been torn beyond repair, and then there was the surgical removal of his ruptured testicle.

For Lima, to abuse her superior power in such a brutal manner would ordinarily have been unthinkable. Except she wouldn't have thought about it. When she became aware of the full extent of the betrayal she shed whatever humanity was left in her. Whether that was instinctive or calculated on her part I didn't know. It was possible that she had identified what was involved in combating the illness, and realized humanity would interfere. There wasn't much left of it after the shit we'd put her through anyway. What remained had been either consciously or subconsciously discarded to allow her to function as a machine.

What she began to use then wasn't just a philosophy that com-bated adversity: in its purest and most brutal form it was a phi-losophy for using adversity, creating it, in order to reach a goal. In the short term Krav Nafshi may be deemed an aggressive coping mechanism, extreme mental combat; but in the long term Total War was the only thing I could compare it to.

April 1992. Jacqueline had invited her best friend's daughter over for the evening. She had warned me that sixteen-year-old Andrena wanted to pick my brains. As it turned out she was writing an essay on the history of Total War.

She was under the impression that Clausewitz, the much-quoted Prussian military theorist, was the father of Total War.

'Clausewitz never actually used the term,' I said. 'What he talked about was *Absolute War*, which was a theoretical concept he never anticipated being reached. It is argued that in the modern age the closest we have ever seen to *Total* or *Absolute War* was the levée en masse that was brought in by Napoleon in the early 1790s, in which he decreed that all Frenchmen and women were to be mobilized in some form for the military cause. This meant that women and children were expected to make tents, equipment, armaments etc. while old men went to the town squares to rally support for the cause.'

Andrena scribbled away on her notepad. 'So who first used the term?' she asked.

'No one can say for certain, but perhaps the first was another German, Erich Ludendorff, who was one of those behind the dusting-off of the Schlieffen Plan in preparation for World War One. His ideas of *Total War* led him to direct that German submarines attack civilian shipping that was supporting the Allies, which eventually led to the Americans entering the war. Many, however, believe that during the American Civil War, Union Army General Sherman's March to the Sea in November and December 1864 was the first instance of a major industrialized power engaging in an explicit strategy of *Total War*. This march not only destroyed the resources required for the South to make war but their heart to continue the war. There was a brutality in the way that the 65,000 Federal troops consumed or destroyed everything in their path that typified Sherman's view of what he called "hard war". "War is cruelty and you cannot refine it."'

Andrena listened as I churned out what I knew of the development of *Total War* in the twentieth century. It was dark when I'd exhausted the subject and Jacqueline drove her home. I finished working on a report and then began getting ready for bed. I looked out of the front window and noticed my wife's car was back in the driveway but the house was remarkably quiet. I went downstairs and called out to her.

Silence greeted me. I walked out to her car and placed the palm of my hand on the bonnet. It was almost cold: she'd been back a while. The moon was covered by clouds but there was just enough light to follow the pathway around the side of the house and into the back garden. There was a strong breeze and the trees made that distinct sound when the wind rushed through them and thousands of leaves brushed against each other. It was the sound I had always loved. Jacqueline loved it too and would often sit on the swing at the end of the garden for hours when the weather was like this. I would always join her and we would talk. Not about anything in particular: we would just enjoy being together. We hadn't been out here for months, and when I saw her silhouette on the swing I realized this was long overdue. I would enjoy tonight.

I thought that as I sat down with my back against the post of the swing. I thought I would enjoy it right up until Jacqueline began speaking.

She spoke gently but her words were cutting nonetheless. 'Why did you have to lecture her, John?'

'Was I lecturing her?'

'Do you really think she's heard of the Schlieffen Plan, or has any idea what dusting off means in that context? But when you started on about the different extremes of Total War you went too far. You went into detail about Sherman, but Sherman wasn't the problem. Describing the Nazi atrocities against innocent civilians during the Second World War: what were you thinking? That you were initiating army recruits into the horrors of war? It was too much for Andrena. She's just turned sixteen, she's only a girl. She barely said a word when I drove her home. It may be in men's upbringing or your make-up that you have the ability to shut your mind to that level of brutality, but you can't excuse it all by quoting Sherman saying "War is cruelty". There is no excuse.'

Jacqueline was right: Sherman wasn't the problem.

When I was around the same age as Andrena I was told the story of a key episode of the Indian Rebellion in 1857: the Siege of Cawnpore. It was the Bibighar Massacre I found most distressing. The siege and artillery bombardment of the British troops, women and children in Cawnpore ended after three weeks when an agreement was made to give the survivors safe passage out by a fleet of boats. There are differing reports as to how the boats caught fire after the survivors had boarded them, but what followed resulted in the slaughter of the remaining British soldiers, bar four who escaped down river. The survivors, one hundred and twenty woman and children, were taken prisoner and herded into a villa, a bibighar, where they were joined by another eighty British and European women, bringing their number up to two hundred. With a column of British troops approaching and reports of them perpetrating violence on Indian villagers, the order was given to execute the women and children. Two volleys were fired into the bibighar but the rebel troops, sickened by the slaughter, refused to fire again. Four of the town's butchers were recruited. Armed with the tools of their trade they entered the bibighar just before sunset. They came out an hour later covered in blood. I could picture the reaction of the women inside when the four butchers dressed in their white aprons forced the doors open and, cleavers in hand, made their way in. I could feel the women's terror. Jacqueline was right to some degree about upbringing, but it was not the all-important factor — they were helpless victims because none of them had been trained to fight. If a percentage of them had been, they would have been totally focused on combat — the fear and terror would not have existed. They were defending their children; with improvised weapons and vastly superior numbers they would have attacked the four butchers from all sides, slaughtered them or died fighting. Instead, without knowing how to fight, they died like cattle and sheep in an abattoir.

'I made a mistake,' I said quietly. 'I forgot her age; she looks so much *older …' I stopped speaking then because the moon had broken out from behind the clouds and I could see my wife's face clearly.*

Jacqueline never made a sound when she cried. Her eyes just filled with tears which would then proceed to stream down her face. Right now her tears were seconds away from spilling over. She was acutely aware of the distress of others, particularly children.

I knelt beside her and gently wrapped my arms around her shoulders. I whispered that she was right, there was no excuse, and that I would visit Andrena tomorrow and apologize.

It would be the last time I would forget the extent of Jacqueline's love of children.

Lima was sleeping when I left the observation room. On the way back to my quarters I looked up at the sky. There wasn't a cloud to be seen. Just as when I was a boy, I was still filled with wonder looking up at the night sky, gazing into infinity. It occurred to me that perhaps I should follow Lima's strategy. I could try to believe that she would get through this. I could view belief in the same way the Greeks viewed infinity. They accepted that with our finite minds we would never understand it, but they still used the concept.

Yet belief wasn't going to be enough; with the cruelty in war comes the madness. Rule Two, combined with denying and distorting reality and using adversity, ensured that Lima would remain on course irrespective of actual reality. Her condition, however, needed medical treatment. This being withheld, Lima was on an irreversible course towards her own death.

I needed to act to ensure she survived. Someone had to break the chain of events that was unfolding. The only way out of this now was through Smith, and he refused to speak to me outside the meetings.

I lay awake all night. I had my own monsters to contend with. Aside from the fear that Lima was going to die was the knowledge that even if somehow she did survive, she would never be the same as when PESRE started.

She was now more machine than human.

Day 59

'It's frustrating,' Smith announced. 'She's embracing the pain and discomfort, and that's what I see as being the hold-up. However, you can't embrace your body betraying you. She will lose confidence, and with it the will to resist. It's purely a question of time. It always is. You see it every day in hospitals: illness wears people down, it destroys confidence; and without belief and self-esteem all that's left is a victim.'

Roberts nodded. I shook my head. Smith glared. 'Johnson, you do not understand the inevitability of loss of confidence,' he said. 'What she is doing may work in theory, but not in practice. Over time with constant negative feedback, she has to lose confidence.'

'She's growing in confidence,' I said.

'Explain.'

'She's fully aware of how important confidence is, and she's systematically building her self-worth and self-belief. She's detached from the physical. The fight is all in her mind. She has direction.'

'Direction?' Roberts was incredulous. 'How can you have direction when there's nowhere to go?'

'She sees anything other than withholding the information as irrelevant. She thinks by believing in recovery she's doing all she can, and that her body will start to work for her,' I said.

'Why? There's no evidence to say belief has any impact. Is there, Smith?'

'Well, that's not entirely true. The placebo and nocebo effects show there are conditions where belief can have a considerable impact. There is a power to belief, but it's an unknown.'

'It's unquantifiable,' I said. 'It doesn't matter if, or how much, her believing is having an effect on her condition. What matters is that she believes it works, and in that understanding she then has a goal. Having a goal to believe gives her direction.'

'Fine. So she has direction; but you can have all the direction you want, when your condition is deteriorating it's not going to count for much. It's denial,' Roberts said.

'I agree,' Smith added. 'Eventually the world she's created will collapse around her. She'll despair. Reality will break her.'

'No: this task, withholding the information, is more important to her than her life. Don't you realize the power that's giving her?'

'It *would* give,' Smith retorted. 'There is evidence that shows there is a power but it's only accessible when life is under immediate threat. With Lima there is no threat to her life; she knows the information she's withholding is worthless. You can't manipulate the mind to make it so significant. I read your report about her rules. Rule One maybe has some meaning, but Rule Two – it's fantasy, something which she may believe in; but for that rule to work she has to trick her mind into not just believing something, but accepting it as true – when it's false. In practice you can't do that.'

'But what if you could?'

'You can't!' Roberts bawled.

I didn't take my eyes off Smith. 'What if you could?'

'You mean by creating the stimuli of a life-or-death situation?'

'Yes.'

'If you were able to create the stimuli internally to use that rule, well, it's hypothetical, because you couldn't just pretend the task was more important than your life. In Lima's situation for it to work, either holding to the principle, i.e. the act of persevering, or the task itself, would have to *be* more important than her life.'

Roberts let out a long sigh as Smith continued. 'If you make either one that important, then the truth of it would effectively be set in stone at a subconscious level. In theory there would be no going back, no deviating from course.'

Roberts said something but I was totally focused on Smith.

'Lima has stumbled on an incredibly powerful principle,' I said. 'The idea of making the completion of a task more important than your life – to die rather than fail. She turned that principle into a rule. She applied the rule to withholding the information. That was easy for her. She's now applying it to combat the illness we put into her by controlling her thoughts. She developed a way to enforce the rule – an extreme form of mental combat that distorts and manipulates and uses everything she can get her mind around. In enforcing the rule she's ensured that the act of persevering towards her goal *is* more important than her life. That means that whatever happens, i.e. reality, is irrelevant. Hell, I don't even know what her reality is any more. From the outset she's been substituting it with her future one.'

Smith sighed again and shook his head. 'Rule Two, you can't–'

'Haven't you listened to the recordings? She's done it already. Rule Two is fixed in place now. You can't break that, and if you can't break the rule you can't break *her*. What she's done is a major part of this experiment.'

Smith and Roberts stared at each other.

'Or is it?' I asked, the truth of the situation sinking in – that the experiment was only interested in methods used to break down, not those used to resist.

'This wasn't supposed to happen,' Roberts explained. 'No one envisaged even the toughest soldier withstanding this kind of pressure; not in an exercise, and certainly not to withhold a piece of worthless information.'

'So, my reports are worthless?'

'No, but I don't think they will be quite as important as you think. Lima's an exception and you can't expect other soldiers to match her standards,' Roberts said. 'Face it, Johnson, she's a freak.'

I looked from Roberts to Smith, who remained silent, holding his head in his hands. 'Did you ever consider it might not be her?' I said.

'What do you mean?' Roberts asked.

'Maybe it's nothing to do with her, but instead it's about the strategies and tactics she's adopting. You don't understand her rules. I don't think you are fully aware of the power of Rule Two. She is; and to enforce it she's sabotaged positives and destroyed alternatives so she has no choice, nowhere else to go but forwards to her goal. Do whatever it takes, die rather than fail.'

'You keep going on about that rule, and this mental combat to enforce the rule. It's far too extreme, it's not living, it's not even fighting, it's–'

'Total War,' I said quietly.

'It's too impractical!' Roberts barked. 'You don't sabotage positives, you hold on to them. It's absurd!'

'It wouldn't be a conscious decision,' Smith said, still holding his head in his hands.

'What?' Roberts asked.

I held my breath. Had Smith finally grasped the implications of what Lima was doing?

'It would be to start with, but if what Johnson says is true, and she's managed to make the act of withholding the information more important than her life, well, from that point onwards the sabotaging would be directed by the subconscious. She would have no conscious control.'

I didn't wait for Roberts to respond. 'Prolonged *extreme* stress resistance. If you're under extreme stress, isn't it natural to use extreme methods to resist? And what would make someone go to such extremes anyway? Things seemed to change after the illness really set in, the day she smashed up the interview room. Betrayal affects people in different ways.'

'What are you implying, Johnson?'

'She put her trust in us and we betrayed that trust. How did you think she would react? She's conditioned and trained to do one thing: to fight. You keep talking about breaking her, but the *her* has gone; all that's left is a machine, stuck on one path, with one programme that is replaying constantly.'

Smith was staring at the table when he spoke. 'You think we'll never get the information. You really believe she'll die first.'

They weren't questions. Smith knew the answers.

'Confidence not only often negates destructive emotions, it makes you think you can do most anything,' I said. 'Her strategy works because she believes it will. It doesn't matter how twisted her logic is or what methods she uses. The reality is her logic is sound but that's not important; what is important is that she's found a way to use pain and adversity, which in turn manufactures drive and confidence, which allows her to persevere with her routine. That routine is allowing her to believe in her future, and that belief is the key, because aside from negating all the fears and doubts that we have been trying to instil in her, it's triggering mechanisms that medical science doesn't fully understand. But also – and here's the killer – her strategy is self-perpetuating, it's feeding itself. All the physical and mental devastation that illness would ordinarily wreak is fuel for her.' I was looking at Roberts but I'd been communicating with Smith from the outset. 'She's changed the rules and she's in her own combat zone. She doesn't allow anything to enter her zone; not even emotions, unless she wants to use them.'

Roberts was obviously waiting for Smith to put up a medical argument, but it wasn't forthcoming; the seed of doubt had been sown by Lima's resistance, and now it seemed Smith had finally grasped the full implications of Rule Two. His lowered head and slumped shoulders were the body language of a beaten man. Roberts saw it: he couldn't hide the hint of panic in his voice. 'About that day, Johnson, the day she went into that fit of destruction: we had her on the edge then; did you ask her about that?'

'Considering the violence surrounding that event, I felt it would be advisable to avoid it, unless she wanted to talk about it.'

'Find out what happened. I want to know why she did it, and what her problem was with the mirrors. You should have asked about this before now. Get in there and find out.'

It was over a month ago, and I still didn't want to bring it up with Lima.

Interview Room

The last few weeks had taken a great toll on Lima physically. Her lightweight trousers and T-shirt drowned her. Two months ago I was mesmerized, but today I didn't want to look at her. Even with the aid of a makeshift stick she struggled to make her way to the chair opposite me. I wanted to help but wouldn't, and it wasn't because of Roberts or protocol but because I knew Lima would hate it.

I went through the normal routine of asking for the information. Lima, as usual, declined. Her speech was noticeably slower and her breathing laboured. I wanted to get this over with as quickly as possible.

'Why did you smash up the room?'

'I needed to destroy something.'

'What?'

'The past: who I was.'

'Is that why you didn't allow the mirrors back in?' I asked

'I didn't want to see the physical deterioration.'

'Isn't that denial?'

'I have to stay focused on the future, not the present. It is an effort to shut out what is in your face the whole time. Having no mirrors just cut down on effort. One thing less to do.'

'This whole thing about believing in the future and your belief working for you – it's just theory – what if it doesn't work? Lima, it's not working.'

'Still you fail to understand. You forget so quickly. The rules; there are only two of them.'

'There's still time to turn this around.' *It's taken too long to get the information. The experiment has failed, you've proved that.* 'Let us get you well, and get you back to your unit.' *The man in charge won't let this go. He'll take it to the end; you're killing yourself for no reason.*

'There is nothing to turn around.'

'Yes, there is.' *There must be friends and family waiting to see you. Yet you keep thinking only of your rules. Why are you being so selfish?*

'I have told you all I can. I have nothing else to say.'

With that she stood up and began the slow walk back to her bed. She was breathing heavily the whole time.

I spent most of the night in the observation room. As I sat looking at Lima on the monitor screen, it dawned on me that my feelings were not so different from those of the male soldiers in the IDF when the women in their unit became wounded. The primordial need to protect her had completely overridden my training. With Lima it was always going to happen – she was just too like Jacqueline.

Today was to be our last conversation. A few hours after the interview had ended she announced to the camera that she wasn't well enough to contribute in interviews and combat the illness.

She had had to choose and her decision would not have been influenced by my calling her selfish. She knew all her actions were terribly selfish. She had made a decision to die rather than surrender the information, with absolutely no consideration for family, friends or members of her unit. As soon as she began enforcing Rule Two all those people were banished from her mind unless she found a way to use them.

The reason she decided to end the interviews was almost certainly the same reason she destroyed the mirrors. She needed to focus on her goal, not tie up her mind in shutting out my attempts to get her to stop.

Just one thing less to do.

The next couple of days I watched her from the monitor but I missed our personal exchanges, I missed sitting across from her. I knew it was no longer a question of how long she could keep going: now it was a question of how long before Smith stepped in. He would, I was sure of it now. As medical officer he would be held responsible if Lima died. During the next meeting three days later he suggested that the experiment be brought to an end. Roberts stalled.

I slept soundly that night, knowing it would only be a matter of a day or two now before Smith enforced his authority as medical officer.

Day 63

I was late getting up, and was just out of the shower when a corporal turned up at my quarters. He had clearly been running and gave me the order to report immediately to the meeting room.

I dressed quickly and seven minutes later walked into the meeting room. Roberts was on his own, sitting in his usual seat.

'Sit down, please, Johnson.'

Please? His entire tone was different, softer, and, as such, very unsettling. I sat and listened.

Jacqueline had been involved in a car accident and was in a coma. Roberts explained that with Lima no longer taking part in the interviews there was no immediate need for me to be here and that I was now on compassionate leave for three weeks. Transport had been laid on; a car and driver were on their way. Roberts was clinical in his efficiency; he recognized what was needed and acted accordingly.

It was about the only time in the last month when I hadn't felt the urge to strangle him.

The hospital was two hundred miles away. With it being immediate next of kin the army classed it as Category A Compassionate, which meant that they would move heaven and earth to get me there in the shortest time possible. Roberts had been emphatic about my being taken to the hospital; he even apologized that no helicopters were available. 'A *very* senior officer, based locally, is currently out of the country. The Divisional Transport Officer has deployed his staff car and driver, who should be here within the next ten minutes.'

Back in my quarters I threw some toiletries and my photocopied file on PESRE into a holdall. I stepped outside to see that the driver had already drawn up and was waiting beside the open back door of the Daimler Double-Six.

Fifteen minutes down the road I saw a garage in the distance.

'Pull in at the garage,' I said.

The driver was experienced; he was more than capable of shifting the big car around the back roads but it wasn't fast enough for me. I felt I was about to implode with frustration, sitting in the back seat. With my world spiralling, I had to feel in control of something. I knew I would be disobeying orders in what I was about to do, but I simply didn't care.

The driver, a corporal in the Royal Corps of Transport, pulled in to the garage forecourt. I asked him to step out of the vehicle.

We stood face to face at the side of the car.

'What are your orders, Corporal?'

'To get you to your destination as quickly as possible, sir.'

'Well, then you need to let me drive, and I am ordering you to do so. If after five minutes you think you can get me there faster I'll pull over and we'll change places. You want to report me, fine: I have no problem with that; otherwise this is between us, and I submit a glowing report on your driving skills ...'

I had no need to continue: the corporal had already started walking round to the passenger side of the Daimler.

Normally it would take over an hour to reach the motorway. We were there around the forty- minute mark. I was so focused on the road, I had barely thought about leaving Lima alone; I knew Smith wouldn't take the fall for this. Lima would be on the correct medication and into her recovery within a week.

When I pulled on to the motorway I floored the accelerator pedal. The Daimler Double-Six was a luxury car, but it was arguably the fastest luxury car in the country. With a Jaguar 6.0-litre engine producing over 300 brake horsepower, when the road was clear we thundered down the outside lane at close to 150 mph. My mind, however, was racing even faster.

When I reached the hospital Jacqueline's condition hadn't changed; still in a coma in intensive care. Her physical injures, particularly the extensive bruising to her right side, were overshadowed by the head injury. The doctors were non-committal. It was a time for waiting and observing.

The sister in charge let me sit by Jacqueline's bedside. Through the night I felt a growing concern. I had never imagined there was a possibility I would outlive her. Why was I here, alive, watching Jacqueline's life slip away? It shouldn't be this way. This was wrong. I should have died on that hill eleven years ago.

The fiercest fighting in the Falklands War took place on Mount Longdon two days before the end of the conflict. At the time I was a platoon sergeant in the regiment I joined as a seventeen-year-old in the early '70s.

The Falklands was a release of tension for those who had served a number of tours in Northern Ireland. There the enemy stayed hidden, and when they did come out they didn't fight in the open: they planted bombs and sneaked away, they hid in crowds of innocent civilians. Northern Ireland was a dirty war where the soldier became caught up in a web of religion, politics and booby traps. The Falklands was crystal clean by comparison. We knew who the enemy was, and where they were. Now we had real targets, legitimate targets. It was a time when we could actually do what we were trained to do without civilians getting in the way. Finally, we had the opportunity to kill the enemy.

Unlike most of the other Argentinian positions on the Falklands, Mount Longdon was defended by a number of well-trained and heavily armed soldiers. Our battalion, the Third Battalion of the Parachute Regiment, was to take the hill, with 2 PARA being held in reserve. It was a dark night, our men falling under machine-gun and sniper fire. There were more British casualties in that assault than in any other engagement during the Falklands War.

The sound of machine-gun fire followed by bullets screaming past your head is bad enough but the sight and sounds of men you know as friends being hit then screaming in agony has a profound effect on you. Your nerves are shredded. When you hear the order to fix bayonets, the sound of the man who shouts it never, ever, leaves you. It haunts your nightmares, it calls out to the primordial instinct inside you to surface. On Mount Longdon, in the middle of the night, it was the order preparing us to run up that hill and kill whoever was in front of us, or be killed trying.

In that situation no two soldiers are affected the same. Some struggle to overcome their fear; with others the fear for their comrades takes over, resulting in acts of great bravery. With a few, there were acts of extreme and untempered violence. I heard talk of one of the men in one of the other platoons, Sergeant George Boyle, whose primordial instincts took over and blocked out all fear, but also any discipline or training on his part. The rumours were contained within a small group, though no one appeared to have witnessed what happened. I knew Boyle, and I'd seen the devastation he could inflict on other human beings with his bare hands, but would still say in his defence that it's not easy to take prisoners when you're caught up in a bayonet charge. You don't just switch off killing mode. It's not that simple.

For my part, I took control of my fear by holding on to my training, counting through the numbers in my mind as I unhooked my bergen, letting it fall to the ground, before I unsheathed the bayonet and clicked it in place at the end of my self-loading rifle. Having discarded what I could that would slow me down, I crouched ready to begin my sprint towards the top of the hill. On the run I zigzagged as I had been trained. Throughout the charge I could hear the sound of the instructors' voices from Aldershot over the sound of machine-gun fire and mortar shells exploding.

A nurse swept in and checked the monitors, then all the lines and fittings connected to Jacqueline. As she left, her hand rested briefly on my forearm.

The company sergeant major did exactly the same thing before closing the lid of the car boot on me in West Belfast fourteen years ago. It was May 1979 and while I remained 3 PARA I was on a two-year attachment to 14 Intelligence Company, specifically East Det, based at Palace Barracks.

We were all in plain clothes. The sergeant in the front of the Ford Consul drove directly to the street in the Ballymurphy where the terrorist suspects were known to reside, and parked up. He then left the car with me in it, armed with a Browning 9mm and a radio to observe what was going on. In '79 an operator from 14 Int cramped in the boot of a car with a tiny hole to look through was the most modern form of spy technology we had available. In this particular street in Belfast it was also an archaic death-trap. If I used the radio I would be heard, and in my cramped position the Browning pistol may have been of use if I was facing one or two hostiles but would prove to be ineffective against any more. If any of the men I was there to spy on suspected a British soldier was hiding in a car boot they would break off the petrol cap, stuff a rag in, put a match to it and stand clear.

As the locals chatted around the car, I observed and listened in silence. Then the talk began to focus on the Consul.

'Here, Colm, you seen this car about?'

'Nah, who got out of it?'

'Lads, did youse see who got out of this?'

I could see them, a handful of ten-year-olds, shaking their heads.

'Well, we'd better have a look, then. Rían, go on in and get the bar at the back of the kitchen. There's a wee torch on the floor too.'

By bar he meant crowbar, and it hit me as soon as I heard the word. They weren't going to open the boot: there was always the risk of a bomb being set off; but with the right tool you could prise open a corner and look inside with the aid of a torch.

The car boot was suddenly bereft of oxygen. I pulled at the collar of my shirt, I couldn't breathe, and when I gasped for breath I tried to stifle it, aware that they must hear my laboured breathing. My mind raced as it tried to identify the right memory from training, but I knew there wasn't one.

There was no training to hold on to now.

For some, their life may flash before their eyes before they die; but I instead was transported back in time to a year earlier...

I could feel the wind's breath as it swept Jacqueline's hair across her face, the sun glinting off it. She brushed the strands back and rested her head on my shoulder. It was sunset and we were alone at the top of Arthur's Seat, the giant hill that overlooked not just Edinburgh but the outlying districts. You were so far above the bustle of the city it was easy to pretend you were in the heart of the countryside.

'So, tell me again, John, what is it you'll be doing on this two-year attachment?'

'Intelligence-gathering, mainly.'

'And that's safer than being on foot patrol in Belfast?'

'Of course.'

'Yeah, well, that's the point that confuses me. If it's a safer job, why, before you even start, do you have to complete a six-month training course with the SAS?'

'It's not so much the SAS, it's just that that particular course is held at Hereford.'

Jacqueline nuzzled her face into the opening at the top of my jacket. 'But if you have to be on the street to gather intelligence, is it not safer to be in uniform?'

'Most of the work will be in an office.'

She pulled back from me. 'Bullshit! John, that's total bullshit and you know it.'

The warm sun had turned cold. I'd been mesmerized by her affection; I had lost focus.

'Why are you always getting into the danger zones? There was no need to volunteer for this.'

I looked out at the breadth of the landscape around us. Why had I tried to deceive her? I knew better than that. But I also knew that the little Jacqueline knew was just touching the surface. Working as part of a detachment of 14 Int would be the most dangerous thing I had ever done.

'Yes, you're right, but you know the plan: I finish this, I could get another promotion; then I apply to transfer to Intelligence and at the same time apply to make the leap to a commissioned officer. We've been working towards this all the time; this attachment merely accelerates it.'

'And what's the point of a plan if you get killed halfway through?'

'I won't.'

'You won't?'

'I won't.'

'Really?' The faintest hint of a smile was glinting in her eyes; the total confidence in my voice had obviously had some impact.

'Really,' I said emphatically.

'Promise me you won't. Promise.'

I placed the edge of my right forefinger under her chin, tilted her head up to face me and looked straight into her eyes, which were burning bright amber. 'I promise,' I whispered.

The sound of the crowbar twisting metal jolted the memory, the flash of daylight broke it…

'Here, Rían, take this and give us the torch.'

I saw the major walking up the path towards my house, a young female officer beside him. That was standard protocol: always have a woman on hand. I saw Jacqueline opening the front door to them, knowing immediately what had happened. She wouldn't let them in, she would stand straight and true as the major went through his speech. As they walked away she would close the door and lean against it, the tears forming, and as they began to fall she would whisper, 'You promised, John, you promised.' Then I watched her life unfolding without me there to protect her. I bit down hard on my hand to stop me from crying out.

Forgive me, Jacqueline. Forgive me.

The monitors beeped, the nurse came in to change Jacqueline's fluid bag. As she worked away in silence I went over the chain of events that led to my surviving that deathtrap.

The precise moment the beam from the torch broke into the car boot, a routine RUC patrol turned the street corner and the group around the car scattered. The RUC radio call was picked up but it had been preceded by one from a helicopter which was assigned to watch over the two 'spy cars' operating that morning. With the RUC patrol car still in the street, the Consul's 'owner' returned. Approaching from the front, he jumped casually into the driving seat, pulled out and drove past the RUC patrol. We had exited the street and were halfway across Belfast before my heartbeat slowed.

The nurse left the room, leaving me alone again with my wife.

I started at her unmoving face, as if I could will her eyelids to flutter. A sign, just one; that was what I wanted.

Why had I survived? How could I survive without her? As the night wore on, the realization that I was going to lose Jacqueline began to overwhelm me. I went from one memory to another, sinking closer and closer to despair. Logic told me I had to pull myself out of it. Lima had told me there was a power to belief, and the phrase 'faith can move mountains' went right back to my childhood. Now sitting next to Jacqueline it didn't seem to matter if it was for me or for someone else; if I could believe, it might help. Besides, I had to feel some form of control; I had to do something. So I tried to believe, but almost everything I understood to be true resisted it.

'You look for proof, and even if you find it, you look for more; you'll never have enough to feel safe.'

'Safe from what?'

'The despair that will hit you if your belief turns out to be false.'

It was just as Lima had said: I was afraid to believe. I prayed, I hoped, but these thoughts didn't allow for belief. Belief was far more powerful than hope. If I had believed I would have let go of hope. How could I have done that? I needed to hold on to hope; it was all I had. Besides, how could I believe if logic opposed it?

So how did Lima believe? I had forgotten already; she wasn't trying to believe, she was merely playing out films of the future she wanted. This was a distinctly separate exercise; and it was based on a different timescale. I had to believe right now. Lima's strategy was long-term; by forced repetition she was working to deceive her brain. She was sidestepping the resistance that I was encountering when I tried to believe. By holding to a strict routine she was brainwashing herself into thinking these future events would take place. It was belief via misdirection. Yet a number of magicians felt that misdirection was a negative term and as such was misleading. They felt that what they were doing was redirecting. If what Lima was doing worked, then it would indeed be redirection.

I didn't have time to redirect my mind, so instead I held on to hope; I nurtured it by convincing myself that Jacqueline was getting the best care, and that I wouldn't leave her side until she came out of this.

But as I looked at her, so frail and vulnerable, the bastion of hope that I had just created began to disintegrate. If only she had been built like Lima, she might have walked away from that accident.

There is a dark time between night and dawn. In the army it is recognized as the time when we are at our most vulnerable to attack. In the field it is called 'Stand-To', short for 'Stand-To-Arms', first used in the trenches in the First World War, where troops took position to repel enemy attack. Anyone who can't sleep is also very aware of this time, when they are open to the demons of their conscience and fears for the future. It is generally accepted as the time when we are most susceptible to despair. Aside from the previous night I hadn't slept properly for almost two months.

I could feel the hopelessness of it all reach inside me. I was nothing without Jacqueline. I couldn't outlive her.

If I did, it wouldn't be for long.

There was something comforting in the thought that if Jacqueline died I would join her quickly. As long as I was with her, that was all that mattered. I leant forward in the chair, leant my head onto the side of her bed, and closed my eyes.

Within a few minutes I was asleep. I dreamt I was back in Northern Ireland, before my attachment to 14 Int.

I was on the last week of a four-month tour with 3 PARA, and we were called to an incident in a bar in the Shankill Road. There had been a bad feeling in the Loyalist area since an IRA bombing the previous week. Tensions were running high, and accusations of lack of action by the police and army were being cast. We surrounded the bar and I was the first man to go in. The sight that greeted me was like a bar brawl out of an old Western movie except that blood was splattered everywhere. Within two seconds I was knocked to the ground by a flying brick intended for someone else. Aside from giving me a major concussion and amnesia, it split my forehead open. An hour later I was in the Medical Reception Station with an army nurse attending the wound. I could feel her cleaning it, telling me that there was no fracture and that everything was all right. Her touch was gentle and as I woke from the dream to the sights of the high- dependency room I could still feel it.

'It's all right, everything is all right,' she whispered. I then realized that everything *was* all right, because this was Jacqueline's voice, and it was her hand that was gently stroking my forehead.

I lifted my head up and smiled. She smiled in return, though it was one of her brave-face smiles. She'd been in a war, but it was over now.

I had no idea then that her war was just about to begin.

Jacqueline spent the next five days in hospital. I was relieved when I was finally allowed to take her home. I thought we would spend the next fortnight together but it became clear that she wanted to deal with this her way, and that meant mostly alone. I occupied myself with writing a draft of the final report. As the days wore on I began to wonder if Smith had in fact intervened. Doubt began to creep in, and I began to worry about Lima.

I still had a full week left of leave, but Jacqueline was eager for me to return to camp. As was I. Each hour I became more concerned about Smith and whatever morals he had left in him. On the day that Jacqueline's sister returned from holiday in Australia I hired a car and left at lunchtime.

Half an hour down the road, I began to question my decision to leave early. My instincts told me to go back. I turned the car around, stopped at a florist and bought a bouquet of pink and white roses. An hour after I'd left I was back at the house.

When I walked into the hall I was going to call out, but the loud music coming from the living room stopped me. Jacqueline didn't play music during the day.

I had always been acutely aware of how good-looking a woman my wife was. I'd never imagined she would have an affair, but I suppose the fear that she might must have been hidden somewhere at the back of my mind because the idea suddenly seized me. All the times I'd phoned and she'd been out now bore down on me, as did her eagerness for me to return to camp. Why had it taken me so long to realize? I felt the walls were closing in as I walked slowly towards the music. I stood at the living-room door for a few seconds, then gently pushed it open. I watched unseen, afraid to breathe, as Jacqueline lay stretched out on the floor, her silent tears rolling out of the corners of her eyes before falling onto the rug.

I ran over to her, dropped to my knees and cradled her in my arms. I carried her upstairs to the bedroom. She didn't look at me, just held her face against my chest. When I reached the bed I gently laid her down and curled up alongside her, wrapping my arms around her. I held her until she stopped crying. She whispered that she was fine now, and that I'd better get back to the camp. I brushed her hair to the side and kissed her forehead.

Downstairs I phoned her sister. She had just returned home from the airport. I explained about the accident and how the trauma was only now affecting Jacqueline. Alison said she would be round in an hour and would stay overnight.

Back upstairs I looked in on Jacqueline; she was sleeping. Not wanting to wake her I quietly sat on the floor with my back leaning against the bed, my head close to hers. I listened to her gentle breathing. It was something I always found soothing; no matter what sort of pressure I was under that sound made me feel instantly at peace. Within five minutes I was asleep.

I was at camp. I was sure I had had this dream before, and it was unfolding in a predictable manner. Yet no matter how hard I tried, I couldn't do anything to change it.

I ran to the complex. The guard was missing. I ran straight in and over to her bunk. She was asleep. I cradled her in my arms and, with the blankets wrapped around her, lifted her up.

We were outside and I was running towards the car park. She weighed so little I carried her easily. I could hear her stirring from her sleep.

'Not far now,' I whispered. But as before my heart sank when I noticed a line of soldiers one hundred yards ahead, blocking our path.

I turned and another line of soldiers appeared. I looked around and all I could see were lines of soldiers, shining flashlights, slowly advancing towards us.

There was no way out. Not this time.

I could feel her hand gently grip my forearm.

I looked down at the woman in my arms, to see Jacqueline looking up at me.

I woke to the sound of Alison's car pulling into the driveway.

I stood, and, with a last look back to confirm that Jacqueline was still asleep, quietly made my way downstairs and met her sister at the front door. I kissed her on the cheek and walked out to the hire car.

Ten minutes later I was on the road out of town. I began to wonder about the dream. I was worried about Lima, yet it was Jacqueline in the dream. It didn't make sense: of the two of them, Lima was the only one who could be in danger now.

They say there's a reason behind your dreams; that it's the subconscious trying to tell you what your conscious has missed. The subconscious doesn't work with logic so it uses association to bring the message across.

Why would Jacqueline be in danger?

The hospital was on the outskirts of town. As I drove there I went through the memories of the last fortnight.

There was nothing; from her discharge from hospital up to today it was all very normal aside from her being a little distant. Today was the only thing abnormal. Why was she playing music that loud through the day? But it wasn't just any music, was it? I recalled the moment I pushed the living-room door open. Only now did the words of the song penetrate my conscious.

I saw it all then, I saw the hopelessness of it, the despair of it, and I wished it had been a man in the room with Jacqueline, I wished in that moment that she had been having an affair.

The song was about a girl called Aubrey and how, although the singer had never known her, he had still loved her. It alluded to a lost love, possibly to a child that had died at birth. The song had such impact that from its release in the early '70s it had, in the US, swapped the assumed gender of the name from male to female.

Five minutes later I was at the hospital. The doctor who had been involved in my wife's care wasn't on, but the nursing sister who'd been in charge was. This was better: I'd spoken to her every day Jacqueline had been in hospital. After a considerable wait I was able to speak to her in her office. I asked when they'd found out and why I hadn't been told.

'It became apparent clinically during her stay here.'

I had caught her off guard and she was trying to keep it vague, but I kept gently applying pressure and it became evident that Jacqueline only found out she was pregnant from her GP the day before the accident, and that when the sister and the house doctor had told her she'd miscarried she'd shown no emotion whatsoever. They would have had no idea how badly she would have taken the news.

'She was very concerned about you,' the sister continued. 'She said that you didn't need any distractions right now. She wanted to tell you in her own way at the right time. She was insistent on this, and naturally we respected her wishes.'

I was numb to it all. We first heard the song at a time when we were planning to have children. Jacqueline immediately said I could choose the name if it was a boy, but if it was a girl she wanted her to be called Aubrey. She would have been so excited about telling me when I returned home on leave.

I should have gone back to see her as soon as I guessed what had happened. When I left the hospital almost two hours had passed. She might have slept for a lot longer, but it was more probable that she was engaged in a conversation with Alison now. Why had I not listened to the words of the song at the time? Why hadn't I checked with the hospital earlier?

The last line of the song, about Aubrey being mine for a day, would haunt me.

There are times when you just can't fix what's broken. I kept telling myself that as I drove along the motorway. I was on autopilot heading back to camp because I couldn't cope. I couldn't handle the knowledge that my wife was breaking apart, the loss of our unborn child, and the uncertainty of what might be happening with Lima. With no real direction I held on to military logic, which justified where I was going: Lima was potentially in the greatest danger and Jacqueline probably needed her sister a lot more than she needed me.

As I drove through the dark time of the night, the logic of it began to sicken me. I needed to turn around and go home, but I wasn't far from camp now. I would arrive there at least an hour before Roberts or Smith would appear. I would quickly see that Lima was fine and immediately head straight home, and stay with my wife for the last week of my leave.

Day 78

I parked up at 0615 and immediately headed over to the complex. The first thing I noticed when I entered the observation room was that all the VCRs were missing. There were a number of stands and monitors around Lima's bunk but no sign of Lima.

Smith was sitting alone in the meeting room, writing.

'What's happened? Where's Lima?'

Smith stared at me for a few seconds before replying. 'The experiment is over. Roberts refused to follow my recommendations. Yesterday evening I contacted the Camp Commandant and explained my concerns. He terminated the experiment immediately.'

'Where's Lima?'

'She's gone.'

'You mean she's dead.'

'Her condition deteriorated rapidly yesterday. I am afraid it's irreversible now. They've taken her to a hospice.'

My hands clenched into fists. 'What's irreversible?'

'Her deterioration.'

'Where's Roberts?'

'He's being returned to his unit under escort. The Camp Commandant is compiling a report, and Roberts will have to answer to that. Doubtless there will be an internal inquiry, and possible charges. I communicated your concerns and request to end PESRE from an early stage to the Commandant; he is aware that you began submitting reports to him weeks ago. Unfortunately they didn't get past the adjutant.'

'You were the one to get past the adjutant. Why did you wait so long? You knew she wouldn't surrender the information.'

'I didn't know. I kept trying to warn–'

'You can't warn someone that arrogant; you needed to act.' I motioned to the paper in front of him. 'Do you think anyone's going to read that?'

'Why, of course.'

'Just pass all the blame on to Roberts.'

He turned and looked directly at me. 'Look, I was just obeying his orders.'

I spoke quietly at first, but my anger increased with each word. 'She was totally committed to this experiment. She really thought she was part of a team trying to make a difference. She contributed in the interviews, she took everything we threw at her and kept going, even after we betrayed her. She took the pain, the deterioration, the distress, seeing her body wither away ... for what? All that pain; it was all for nothing. And of course you weren't involved, you just obeyed orders.'

'You were there when I recommended that the experiment be terminated. You heard me!' Smith spoke loudly, but there was desperation in his voice.

I shook my head, fully aware of the violence that was coming, even though part of me knew it wasn't just his fault. It was all our faults. It was my fault for being weak. The army's for allowing someone like Roberts to be in charge. And it was Lima's fault, her inability to deviate from her rules. I told her how this would end but everything was irrelevant to her, except her rules and her orders: withhold the information. She gave up nothing from the outset: her defiance pitted against Roberts's arrogance. I saw the same group of images I'd seen too often: Lima collapsing, trying to stand, vomiting, leaning on the wall, then, after struggling to her feet, shuffling back to her bunk. Pulling the covers slowly over her as if the thin cotton could in some way replace the years of physical conditioning we'd stripped away. I looked at Smith. The change in my voice must have been like a warning siren to him: he had positioned himself so that the giant table was between us.

I placed the palm of my left hand in the centre of the table and swung my legs over, like a gymnast on the pommel horse. The speed of the move took Smith by surprise and he scurried into a corner, but I was on him in a second, grasping his shirt and two handfuls of skin beneath it, pulling him towards me, then driving him back hard into the wall. His eyes glared wide with shock. I held him there, my grip tightening, my true self finally dominating. I yearned to reach deep inside him and rip the falseness out, his pretend code of medical ethics, cleanse him of his hypocrisy. Instead I pressed my left forearm against his throat, forcing his head up the wall, and reached down with my right hand and grasped between his legs. Now I focused my entire being on tightening that hand into a fist. Smith's wail was drowned out by my own yelling. My face inches away from his.

'WHAT'S IRREVERSIBLE? WHAT THE FUCK DID YOU PUT INTO HER?'

There was an abrupt knock on the door. Smith's scream doubled in volume and part of me must have known it would bring in whoever was outside, but I couldn't stop.

I felt a hand gently rest on my shoulder.

After a few seconds I released my grip. I turned to find myself looking at a heavily built staff sergeant. His face was relatively young but his eyes were ancient. I knew that look: too many tours in Northern Ireland. He instructed the two soldiers waiting at the door to take Smith outside. The sergeant didn't speak; he just nodded and held out an envelope. None of the camp's staff knew the details of PESRE, but with the Commandant's dramatic intervention a few key personnel would have some idea of what had happened. Smith may well put in a complaint against me, but would he find any witnesses? Would he want to draw any more attention to himself when his actions had been so unethical? I was past caring.

I looked down at the envelope, studying the name on it. For the last two weeks I'd been using my own name. When I looked up the room was empty. I walked into the interview room, sat down on Lima's bunk, and opened the envelope.

My posting orders, effective immediate upon my return: Belfast. There had been eighty-nine conflict-related deaths in Northern Ireland the previous year, and Belfast was still the hot spot.

I crushed the paper in my hand. I would phone Jacqueline as soon as I arrived, but I wouldn't see her for months.

I desperately needed to get home but I was trapped in military law and protocol now. Orders – you disobey them, you get locked up. I rubbed my eyes with my thumb and forefinger as I struggled to accept the reality of my mistake in coming back to camp. To accept that I had, in any way, betrayed Jacqueline was going to be too difficult.

I shut it out. I pretended it hadn't happened.

I looked around the room, at the table and the bare grey walls where the mirrors had been. Lima. I had been looking forward to seeing her. Something else I had to bury.

That would make two graves this morning.

I ran the palm of my hand in an arc over the bed, smoothing the crumpled sheet out, perhaps as a way of saying goodbye, a final wave farewell. My hand drifted under the pillow and touched something with a sharp edge.

I looked up to see two corporals standing inside the doorway, the one at the front braced to attention.

'We've been ordered to clear this area, sir, if you could please step outside.'

That was a thing about the army: they didn't give you time to get nostalgic, or think about what you'd done wrong; they just moved you on.

At the guardroom I had to hand over the file, all my reports, and then make the usual declaration. It was routine: the punishment for breaking the Official Secrets Act was so severe it was usually an effective deterrent.

But I'd already broken it.

I had left the photocopied file at my house.

Now, twenty years later, I was looking at that file again.

Where was the start point? Who had come up with the idea of PESRE, and why had Lima been selected?

I still had no clear answers. At the time I assumed it was an experiment to find the quickest way of breaking suspected IRA terrorists without the use of anything that could be regarded as torture. With Jacqueline's miscarriage, and Lima's death, I had shut out the entire episode. But now, looking at it in relation to the development of enhanced interrogation techniques after the terror attacks of 9/11, I was struck by the waste of it. The counter-interrogation techniques of SERE that had been reverse-engineered by Mitchell and Jessen encompassed all practical and theoretical measures required to prepare personnel for isolation, interrogation and recovery. A lot of money had been, and still is, spent on teaching these techniques to members of the military who would probably never have to use them. Yet no training was necessary for something as simple as Krav Nafshi. All anyone had to know were the rules and the fundamental principles. It was that simple. However, the extreme mental combat that had been the only product of PESRE had been buried at source because high-ranking officials would be held accountable. It had been more than an embarrassment for British Military Intelligence – a debacle that shone a bright light on major character flaws in a senior officer, and resulted in the abuse and death of a female IDF volunteer. If it had gone public, no one involved would have escaped unscathed.

Now, retired from the army, I viewed PESRE in relation to combating illness as opposed to obtaining or withholding information. I wondered if a form of mental combat could be of benefit to at least some of the masses who were vulnerable to the prolonged extreme stress of serious illness. Unlike the military personnel who were taught techniques to prepare them for whatever might happen – in the remote chance they found themselves in enemy territory – those diagnosed with a life-threatening illness were already in similar territory, yet no consideration was given to advising them on even the most basic techniques to combat its terrors.

Why the oversight? But then, oversight is the wrong word. The extent of the bias towards medication as a result of the massive funding from pharmaceutical companies partly explains it. Business is business, after all, and it is standard practice to eliminate the competition. One of the greatest threats to jobs in the pharmaceutical industry and the medical profession would come from self-healing.

The National Health Service simply is not prepared to promote the idea of any form of mental combat, let alone one akin to Total War where every possible measure is taken to destroy the enemy. They hold to the principle that surgery and medication will do the job, and if not, then there is little or nothing anyone as an individual can do to alter the outcome. It is a major failing: a fight is a fight, irrespective of the arena, and confidence in all fights is crucial. Where boxing training camps are specifically designed to manufacture a fighter's ego, hospitals are designed to manufacture sheep that are easy to manage.

The problem is a fundamental one: sheep don't fight.

Massive sums are being spent on medical research yet, in comparison, next to nothing is spent on researching the potential of the human mind. A valuable resource, a resource of immeasurable power, lies dormant and unused ... wasted.

Yet there were huge dangers with a form of mental combat like Krav Nafshi that was created to enforce something as unforgiving as Rule Two. Embracing pain where warning signals were deliberately switched off could easily prove fatal. It would be abhorrent to most: any philosophy designed to make people feel shame, who may then die in that shame because they had been unable to hold to the routine, would be deemed inhumane. Even if it was clear that this extreme form of mental combat was for the young who wanted nothing other than to fight and were prepared to risk everything, it would be forcefully resisted by institutions. Accusations of cruelty would be cast. People would always say, 'No. You just can't put that responsibility on anyone. You can't offer a method of combat as harsh as this without proof that it works; and even if there was proof, it's wrong for people to berate themselves and induce shame and guilt, and set themselves up for terrible despair through belief, which, unless accompanied by a favourable prognosis, will most probably turn out to be false.'

They may be right, yet there was still a part of me that wanted to publish the findings, if only to give people the choice for themselves. The physical and mental power that is available when life is under immediate threat is immense, and ordinarily that is the only time it would be available. But Lima had found a way of applying Rule Two, tapping into that power and controlling her thoughts.

There could be no multitasking, though. Social interaction would become almost impossible with this level of focus. You would quickly find that isolation was the only way to avoid distractions and apply the rule in its purest form. Isolation afforded greater control. Currently the tendency is for people diagnosed with serious illness to do everything they can to hold on to their normal lifestyle. They see that as fighting, by not letting the illness take anything away from them. Mental combat would simply deem a normal lifestyle as irrelevant, scrapping it in favour of one more conducive to applying the rules and holding to the routine.

Rule Two had allowed Lima to succeed in withholding the information; but only at the potential cost of the rule – her life. She was, then, an example of the terrible implications of applying and enforcing the rule.

As much as I wanted something positive to come out of PESRE, Krav Nafshi was simply too dangerous.

Officially Lima's death would have been recorded as an accident in training. I didn't hear anything about the internal investigation or what happened to Roberts or if any action was taken against Smith. I had buried it deep, and it would have stayed buried if, earlier today, I had gone for petrol a few minutes later.

Just before closing the file I reached inside and my fingers touched the same thing that they had twenty years ago when I'd reached under Lima's pillow. I found myself holding the green and black cord that had been wrapped around the back of her neck and the thin rectangular piece of metal that had lain against her chest.

Twenty years ago I hadn't had time to immerse myself in the emotions that went with holding the object that had touched Lima for almost every hour of her adult life. This diskit was her identity to the IDF, but more importantly, to her. And now, holding the essence of her in my hand, I missed the woman. I missed the way she stroked strands of her hair across her forehead, I missed her smile, I missed the flashing of amber in her brown eyes. Then I realized what I was missing were all the things that reminded me of Jacqueline when she was young, before PESRE, before the accident when everything fell apart.

Was this diskit all that remained of Lima? It couldn't be; there would be family photographs somewhere, someone who still had at least one of her uniforms and kept it safe. What had they told her family? They wouldn't have sent her body home. If her family had opened the casket and seen her emaciated body they would have known this was no accident in training. What had the army done? They couldn't have just told her family and flown them in to see her – there would have been a public inquiry. I hadn't heard anything, because I'd never asked. I had just assumed after what Smith had said that...

It had always been an assumption. In shutting out almost three months of my life, I'd never checked. My mind lurched back a few hours to the service station. Fifteen feet. That was the distance between us. When she walked out of the kiosk her name escaped my lips before I could stop myself.

'Lima.'

She stared straight at me. I hadn't changed so much in those years. She didn't know me. It wasn't her. How could it be? It was like a dream I used to have when I was younger. In it I was immersed in a love that was so deep and pure that in the half-light as I was waking I would try desperately to hold on to the dream. I couldn't bear that this love would be lost, but I was also trying to identify who the woman was in the dream. Who is this great love? Then as my conscious surfaced and I really started to wake up, reality tore her away from me and I realized that's all it was. A dream.

She walked across the forecourt and stood at the pickup, the sun setting behind her. She opened the door, and just before getting in turned towards me. She smiled, shook her head slowly and said something, but with another car's engine revving I didn't hear it.

I replayed the moment again in slow motion.

I could feel the hairs on the back of my neck rise up.

I played it again.

And again.

At the end of the tenth replay I heard Jacqueline at the top of the spiral staircase. I glanced at my watch: it was just after three. The last six hours had disappeared.

'Are you still working?' Her voice was different, frightened.

'Are you okay?' I asked softly.

'Just a bad dream. I'm okay.'

Another nightmare. And she wasn't okay. I closed the file.

By the time I'd made my way up the stairs Jacqueline was sitting on the edge of the bed.

I quickly stripped off my clothes and knelt behind her. Leaning over, I switched the bedside light off.

'Don't. Leave it …'

I whispered in her ear that there was nothing to be afraid of. It was dark but I could sense her looking at me questioningly. I held my right hand at the side of her face, my fingertips barely touching her cheek, then moved my hand slowly backwards, running my fingers through her hair. I ran my forefinger along the line of her cheekbones. I leaned forwards; my lips brushed her eyelids, eyebrows, her forehead, her jawline, the side of her neck. She lifted her arms up towards me but I caught them, placing them back down at her side. Maybe it was the nearness of the nightmare, but tonight she let me reach out to her, she let me take control, and my fingertips traced the curves of her face, her neck and her shoulders.

The hands that had broken so many things had found a sensitivity that had been hidden all my life. They glided over her body. She began to respond, and I could hear her legs brushing against the sheets.

My touch became even lighter, and slower. I held her with a tenderness that I didn't know I possessed. It wasn't sex. We didn't make love that night. I didn't let her do anything. I made love to her as if in a dream. As if it was the first and last time. The only time I would ever make love in my life. And I wanted it to be as slow as possible. I wanted it to last for ever. As if it had to; because it might just have to last a lifetime.

Afterwards, with her arms around me, she whispered into my neck, 'What happened to ...'

She was asleep before she'd finished the sentence.

I lay unmoving, looking at the shadows. I lifted my watch from the bedside table. Almost three hours had passed since I was in the basement. So much had happened and I didn't know what would happen with Jacqueline now. Last night was my way of trying to mend the past, in the hope that we could start again. We might, it was possible; last night had changed things.

But there was more to last night than mending the past. It was not my wife I made love to, but the Jacqueline of twenty years ago: the Jacqueline that I thought was lost for ever, whom I'd glimpsed again yesterday in a woman who had barely aged a day in those twenty years.

I replayed the scene at the service station for the eleventh time.

When she walked out of the kiosk her name escaped my lips before I could stop myself.

She stared straight at me, then walked across the forecourt and stood at the pickup. The sun was behind her; she opened the door, and just before getting in turned towards me. She smiled, shook her head slowly and said something. I didn't hear it, not because of the noise from a car engine, but because she'd mouthed the word.

Emma.

It wasn't a Jewish name, but the name of the wife of the IDF's first general, David Marcus, was Emma. He had a kibbutz, an area in Tel Aviv and several streets named after him. Maybe there was another reason, though it seemed feasible that some baby girls would be named after his wife.

I watched the white pickup pull away; I stood in the same spot unmoving, following its tail lights until they disappeared over the horizon.

I found myself lost in that dream again, wondering if I'd ever wake up now.

The dream didn't last long. When I woke around midday Jacqueline had gone. It had been a wild, crazy dream to think that because Lima, or rather Emma, was alive, and had returned after twenty years of my thinking she was dead, the same would apply to Jacqueline.

I found a note left on the kitchen table, my wife addressing the logistical problems first, saying her sister would collect the rest of her things. She went on to say that she still loved me, but it was too painful to stay with me. She didn't say why; she didn't know that I knew I was a constant reminder.

I had never told her I knew about the miscarriage; I had always been waiting for her to tell me in her own time. I had used it as an excuse for too long. I had shut it out, just as I'd shut out the seventy-eight days of PESRE.

There are some mistakes you never stop paying for.

Epilogue

It's been over six months since Jacqueline left. One hundred and ninety-two days. Today is the first day that has been bearable.

It's one in the morning, and I am sitting beside the swing at the end of the garden. On my lap is a copy of the book Emma had taken her rules from, the biography of Joseph Greenstein. Sleep will be impossible tonight as I try to come to terms with what I've read. At the moment I'm trying to make sense of how Greenstein's principles fitted in not just to Emma's strategy but the bigger picture of the experiment itself and my decision not to publish the results.

Where the principles were applied by Greenstein over a brief moment of time, usually a few seconds, Emma had applied them over months, periods they simply weren't intended for. She hadn't even adapted them, instead applying cruel tactics to keep them in their strict form. The irony was that the principles that had formed her rules had come from a man who had not an ounce of hypocrisy or cruelty in him. Greenstein's life and principles were as straight and true as the thick metal bars and spikes he held in his hands before applying the principles and bending them into trinkets. Emma, finding herself trapped in a rotting bog of hypocrisy and oppression, had fought her way out by doing whatever it took to hold to the purity of those principles.

I saw everything in the book that she had seen, the truth in a story that was beyond anything I'd ever heard of. The Jewish strongman had indeed held aeroplanes back with his hair, and bent iron bars using his mind. I refused to argue using logic any more. I just accepted that there is a power to belief that is way beyond logic, a higher power that I will never understand.

Is that not reason enough to publish the results of PESRE? For all the cruelty that Emma had introduced in order to enforce Rule Two, all the dangers and risks involved in a philosophy which thrives off pain and adversity, which is all wrong for day-to-day living and can be sure of creating nothing other than potential despair – is it enough reason?

It is my decision because I alone will have to face the backlash from anyone who reads the results. Would the risks and great sacrifice necessary to apply and enforce Rule Two, and the implications of the rule, be fully understood? The rule worked because the mental combat that enforced it effectively destroyed everything in life other than the goal. For whoever used the rule, if the goal they strove towards wasn't attained, their life would be spent striving for something that was beyond their reach. Any attempts to alter course would be sabotaged; there would be no going back, ever.

I gaze up at a cloudless night sky, recalling Greenstein's words near the end of the book.

'No man has limits, except in his own mind. Look up, what do you see? Stars, planets, whirling infinity, with no beginning and no end. Enough to make a man lose his mind.'

He was right: there are no limits, only those that logic binds us to, to keep us sane. Emma was also right when she told me not to complicate things. Her routine was as basic as you could get, yet it built confidence and drive and redirected the mind into believing in a positive future, and when you're struggling to cope with any form of adversity you need things to be simple.

Perhaps I can find a less direct way of publishing the findings, but there is something more pressing. I open the cover of the book and take out the other thing I've read today: a letter that arrived from Belgium this morning, Jacqueline's handwriting unmistakeable. I've read it so many times I almost know it by heart. In it she talks about a lot of things, one being the remote possibility of her returning to the UK.

I had been numb when she left, but it wore off after a few hours; then I felt the terrible loss, the permanency of it. It was as if my heart had been ripped out, and for the last six months I had been slowly bleeding to death.

I should have known it would be like this. She was so like Emma in some respects, yet so different: where Jacqueline carried the great burden of the loss of our child, Emma would have severed her maternal side in an instant. How I admired her for being so ruthless in order to survive. From a military perspective her tactics were faultless: she was the ultimate soldier. Where she had barely aged in twenty years, Jacqueline had, and it had happened very quickly. When a woman experiences great loss, the depth of sadness is written all over their face, especially in their eyes, and they possess a beauty that they would never have otherwise. The greater the sadness, the greater their beauty; and Jacqueline's beauty was staggering.

Every day I yearned to wrap my arms around her. She wouldn't let me, though, and now, having wrenched the door open on what had taken place, I knew why she felt she needed to go through that pain by herself. She was so insistent on preventing the hospital staff from telling me because she *never* wanted me to know. As much as she wanted a child, she knew I wanted one even more. She kept the secret to herself because she was determined to protect me. She took on the pain for both of us, fully aware that it might destroy her.

She had, from the beginning, been my right arm, my true friend; and, knowing what I know now, my devoted protector. Yet part of me must have known, right from the moment I walked in on her crying, because in all the years since then, when the sadness cast a beautiful shadow over the amber in her eyes, I had never once stopped loving her, not for a moment. What was true decades ago was even more true today – I would walk a lot further than thirty miles just to see her face.

What have I learnt over those years? It seemed the most important thing had come from Emma. They had tried to break her and failed, because she had applied Rule Two.

Now, without Jacqueline, it feels as if life is trying to break me.

What is the start point?

An image, a film, a future.

I stand and walk inside the house. I sit at my desk and start writing to her, the old-fashioned way, the way love letters are written, in longhand. As I write I visualize her coming off the plane. I see her smiling as she walks towards me; I look in her eyes and see the amber burning again. I feel her arms wrap tightly around me.

I have direction. I will play back that film every day as often as I can. I shall not waver.

And the danger?

There is none, for the same reason enforcing the rule will be easy: without her, I have nothing left to lose.

www.extremementalcombat.com

Copyright Acknowledgement

Acknowledgements

For their invaluable assistance and encouragement I thank Major (Retd) Ian Johnson, Dugald McCallum, Robert McCall, Darren Newbold, Julie Christie, Catherine Deveney and especially for editing and proofreading, Jenny Drewery.